TANGLEWOOD ANIMAL PARK

Baby Zebra Rescue

"Is it a boy or a girl?" Zoe asked, as the baby zebra foal tried to climb onto its spindly legs and failed. It looked so cute and wobbly and adorable.

"A boy," Mr. Fox said. "Actually, we were just wondering whether you and Oliver could think of a name for him."

"You were?" Zoe exclaimed. "I'd love that!"

For Paradise Wildlife Park,
where it all began.

First published in the UK in 2016 by Usborne Publishing Ltd.,
Usborne House, 83-85 Saffron Hill, London EC1N 8RT, England.
www.usborne.com

Cover and inside illustrations by Chuck Groenink.
Illustrations copyright © Usborne Publishing Ltd., 2016

The name Usborne and the devices 🔱🌂 are Trade Marks of
Usborne Publishing Ltd.

A CIP catalogue record for this book is available from the British Library.
This edition published in America in 2017 AE.

PB ISBN 9780794540463   ALB ISBN 9781601304278

JFMAM JASOND/18 03898/6
Printed in China.

Everybody's Talking About
TANGLEWOOD ANIMAL PARK!

"I love it! 1,000 out of 10!" *Finley ☺, age 8*

"Outstandingly gripping"
Daniel, age 8

"I did not want to put it down because I did not want the fun to end."
Dior, age 8

"I love reading about all of the animals. The book makes me want to go and visit Tanglewood."
Freya, age 6

"This is a roarsome book! I love it."

"I really loved reading this book. 10/10." *Holly, age 9*

"I just could not take my eyes off this book. It reminds me so much about myself and my love for animals, just like Zoe!"
Lila, age 10

"I think this book is the best book I have ever read." *Ava, age 6*

"Ridha, age 8"

"I'd love to live with the main character Zoe. I will be telling all my friends to read this book."
Charlotte, age 9

"When I read about Flash the zebra being born it made me feel emotional."
Leila, age 8

"This book was amazingly cool!!!"

"I wish I lived at Tanglewood like Zoe. This book was amazingly cool!!!"

Chapter One

"Tanglewood Animal Park next right!"

Zoe Fox pointed out of the front windshield to a gap in the trees ahead, her voice quivering with anticipation. Her four-year-old brother, Rory, bounced around on the seat beside her and she knew he was just as excited as she was. Even Mom looked up eagerly and she'd been to Tanglewood plenty of times already. *But it wasn't every day you moved into your very own zoo,* Zoe thought, as Dad stopped the car in front of the entrance. Two tall iron gates blocked the way, flanked on each side by a sandstone pillar. On top of the pillars, Zoe saw two carved lions facing each other, caught mid-roar, and beyond them, a deserted road winding through the woods into the distance.

"Wow," Zoe breathed, a thrill of delight chasing up and down her spine.

As entrances went it was pretty grand and a million miles away from the neatly painted red front door of their old terraced house.

Mr. Fox held up a remote control and pressed a button. A groaning, whirring noise filled the air and the gates slowly parted.

"Wait until you see Tanglewood Manor itself," he said. "It's going to knock your leopard-print socks off."

Zoe hugged herself tight with glee – she couldn't

wait to see it. But most of all, she was looking forward to meeting her new neighbors: the animals. She knew there were definitely ring-tailed lemurs, plus lions and zebras. The lemurs were her favorites, though; she couldn't wait to get to know them. Before buying Tanglewood, her dad had been Head Keeper at a big city zoo and her mom had worked there too, so Zoe was used to being around all kinds of animals. But she'd never lived right in the middle of an actual zoo before. Their very own zoo!

As they passed through the open gates, Zoe buzzed her window down and breathed in the hot August air. Now that she was closer, she could see the metalwork was dotted with orange rust. She was surprised and a little bit shocked: *that would never have been allowed at the old zoo*, she thought, picturing the immaculate ironwork she knew so well. Her parents had already warned her that there was a lot to be done at Tanglewood – the previous owners had been a big company who'd run things on a shoestring before eventually closing the park down and selling it to the Fox family. They planned a grand reopening in two weeks' time. If everything was ready…

More trees lined the road after the gates, curving in an emerald arch over their heads. Zoe craned her neck to see around the bend, eager for her first glimpse of the manor. And then the car rounded another bend and an enormous red-bricked building appeared before them.

"Oh!" Zoe gasped in astonishment. "It's huge!"

"Tall," Rory agreed.

Their mother glanced backwards, her eyes gleaming. "Do you like it?"

Zoe nodded vigorously, her gaze fixed on the manor. It was much older than she'd been expecting – it had vaulted windows and turrets and what looked suspiciously like a gargoyle peering down from the edge of the gray slate roof tiles. Wooden beams blackened with age cut into the red bricks in symmetrical patterns. Zoe felt as though she'd slipped hundreds of years into the past.

The car crunched to a halt on the gravel outside

the oak front door. Zoe clambered out, ignoring Rory's indignant squawks at being stuck in his car seat. She walked forwards, gazing around her in wonder.

"Don't worry about the missing tiles on the roof," Dad said. "The builders are going to fix them tomorrow."

Zoe peered upwards. Now that she looked more closely, she could see one or two black areas among the gray tiles. And the roof wasn't the only thing in need of attention – a few windowpanes had cracks in them. *The manor house might be bigger than their old home but it was nowhere near as neat and tidy*, Zoe thought, with an unexpected pang of homesickness.

The front door opened with a creak and a man wearing shorts and muddy green rubber boots walked out. Slouching behind him was a boy of around eleven with dark-blond hair and freckles, wearing a T-shirt with a snarling tiger on the front. And following him was a small group of men and women of all ages, some in green polo shirts, a few in paint-spattered overalls and one lady wearing a black-and-white checkered apron. They gathered around Zoe and her family and began to clap.

Zoe gazed at the smiling faces. This couldn't be everyone who worked at the park – when it was full, her parents had said Tanglewood would be home to more than 350 different animals. Surely they'd need a lot more people to look after them all?

"Hello again," the man said, striding towards them as the applause died down. "Officially – welcome to Tanglewood."

Dad shook his hand. "Thanks, Max. I'd like to introduce my daughter, Zoe, and her little brother, Rory. Zoe, this is Max Chambers, Tanglewood's Chief Vet. He oversees the care of all our animals and runs the Tanglewood medical center."

"Very pleased to meet you," Max replied, his face crinkling into a smile as he solemnly shook their hands. "This is my son, Oliver."

Zoe looked at the boy expectantly. Her parents had told her Max had a son who lived at Tanglewood too. But instead of smiling like his father, Oliver gave her a dead-eyed stare.

"Cool T-shirt," Zoe said, stepping forwards. She held up her tiger-print backpack. "It matches my bag."

Oliver thrust both hands into the pockets of his jeans, looking bored. "Whatever."

"Oliver," Max warned. "Be polite."

The boy grunted. "I've got to go and clean out the zebra enclosure."

Without another word, he turned his back on them all and crunched across the gravel. Max sighed as he disappeared around the corner of the house. "Sorry. He's not normally so rude."

"I understand," Zoe's dad said. "It's a big adjustment. He'll come around."

Zoe stared after Oliver. They were both starting a new school in September, in the same grade, and Zoe had been hoping he would be a friendly face while she found her feet. But from the way he'd acted, she wasn't sure he even knew what the word *friendly* meant. She sighed as another pang of homesickness squeezed at her stomach. The busy city streets, crowded buses and familiar sights of her hometown seemed very far away now. Her friends felt far away too. Even though she could message them whenever she wanted, the long distance made visits unlikely, at least for a while.

Zoe looked around at the rest of the staff – they seemed friendly and smiled when they caught her eye. And then she heard the distant but unmistakable sound of a lion's roar and her homesickness melted away, replaced by a flurry of excitement. That wasn't any old lion, it was her brand-new next-door neighbor. In fact, Tanglewood was full of animals just like him, waiting for Zoe to get to know them. She couldn't wait!

Chapter Two

The first thing Zoe noticed inside the manor was the grand staircase that swept around one corner of the wood-paneled hall and vanished upstairs.

"What's my room like?" she asked, feeling her exhilaration start to grow again. "Does it have a four-poster bed?"

Mom laughed. "No, you'll sleep in your own bed, silly. Come on, let's give you the tour."

"Actually, I thought you might like to come and

say hello to our latest arrivals first," Max said.

Dad tipped his head to the side quizzically. "Not the snow leopards?"

Max nodded. "They're in their den, ready to be released. I wanted to wait until you got here."

Zoe saw her parents exchange glances over her head. Her mother worked as an animal habitat designer and had spent weeks working on a new environmentally-friendly enclosure for the snow leopards. But Zoe knew what was coming next – *play with your brother while we do something interesting*. She thought she might implode with disappointment if they left her behind. "Please can we come?"

"Please?" begged Rory. "I want to see the snow leopards too."

Their father hesitated and Zoe held her breath. The big cats were often the most dangerous animals in any zoo and she knew they needed very careful handling. But surely her parents wouldn't say no to a quick peek from outside? Not on their very first day?

"I don't think—" Dad started to say, but Max interrupted him.

"Actually, the sooner the snow leopards get used to crowds, the better. So it might be quite helpful if Zoe and Rory came along. I could give them a tour of Tanglewood, introduce them to some of our other animals along the way?"

"You'll both have to be really quiet," Dad warned. "No jumping around."

Zoe shook her head, wondering if her father had forgotten she'd be twelve in October. Beside her, Rory put his finger on his lips as though he wanted to prove how quiet he could be.

"Okay," Mom said. "Let's leave our bags here and look around the house later."

Zoe didn't need to be told twice. She dropped her backpack to the criss-crossed wooden floor and beamed at Rory, seeing the enthusiasm on his face. This was it, the start of their Tanglewood adventure, where they'd get to meet their brand-new animal neighbors. Grabbing her little brother's hand, she followed Max and her parents towards the front door. It looked as though life at the park would be even more thrilling than she'd dreamed.

Inside the park, there were things being dug up, or built, or knocked down everywhere Zoe looked. Big wooden fences blocked off some areas, while excavators trundled along the paths between the enclosures. The rumble of machinery was constant – she was amazed the animals weren't disturbed.

"Most of the animals have been temporarily rehomed on the other side of the park," Max called over his shoulder, seeming to read her mind. "We'll bring them back here once the work is finished."

Zoe nodded. There was so much going on – her parents were going to have their hands full getting ready for the grand opening in just a few weeks' time. At least there was plenty to keep herself and Rory busy – she couldn't wait to get stuck into helping with the animals.

She squeezed her little brother's hand. "Look, Rory, it's the reptile house."

They peered through the darkened glass doors, hoping to catch a glimpse of the snakes and lizards inside. Zoe knew they had several large pythons and a boa constrictor and she could hardly wait to see them. But right now, she had something white and much furrier on her mind.

"How old are the snow leopards?" she asked, hurrying to catch up with the adults and tugging Rory along with her. "What are their names?"

"They're sisters from the same litter, so they're both three years old," Dad said. "One is named Minty and the other is Tara. What can you tell me about their natural habitat?"

This was a game they often played – Zoe was so creature-crazy that she knew all kinds of animal facts. But it was hard to concentrate when they were walking past so many amazing animal enclosures, even if most of the residents weren't at home. Zoe frowned.

"Um…they like mountains but will live in grass and shrublands if they're high enough. I think they come from Asia and they're carnivores so they eat meat, probably sheep and goats. Um…"

"They like snow," Rory put in solemnly. "That's why they're called snow leopards."

Everyone laughed.

"That's right," Mom said, ruffling Rory's hair. "Although we don't get much snow around here so I've had to be creative with their new habitat."

The noise and disruption of the excavators faded away as they walked further into the park. It was much bigger than Zoe had expected. The enclosures they were passing now looked like they were being cleaned up – there were wheelbarrows full of branches and plant clippings everywhere. And most importantly of all, these enclosures had residents.

"Oh!" Zoe squeaked as she caught the flash of a black-and-white tail amongst a jumble of ropes and tall trees. "Are those the ring-tailed lemurs?"

"That's right," Max said. "I hear they're your favorites."

Zoe nodded so hard she thought her head might fall off. "Oh, yes! At Dad's old work, I used to go and feed them sometimes. I love it when they sit on your shoulder and curl their tail around your neck."

She stopped and peered through the glass, watching as two lemurs chased each other along the ropes and up into the trees.

Max grinned. "They're not always cute, though. Have you ever seen the males having a stink fight?" He wrinkled up his nose. "They wipe their scent glands on their tails and wave them over their heads at each other until one of them gives in!"

"Thank goodness our noses can't smell that," Mrs. Fox said. "But there'll be plenty of time for you to get to know our lemurs, Zoe. Their keeper, Mizbah, has already offered to introduce you."

Zoe felt her eyes widen. "Really? When?"

Her mother smiled. "Soon, I promise."

With a final eager glance at her favorite creatures,

Zoe followed her parents along the path. Not far from the lemur enclosure was the petting zoo, home to Tanglewood's goats, sheep and rabbits, as well as the guinea pigs. But Zoe's attention was caught by the animal *behind* the guinea-pig run. Standing in front of a small stable, in a field tucked a little way from the main path, was the roundest zebra Zoe had ever seen. Oliver was beside her, a wooden dandy brush in his hand, and behind him was one of the keepers. Zoe smiled and waved when she saw them but Oliver ignored her. He kept sweeping the brush along the zebra's striped neck, his actions careful and sure. *Maybe he was just shy around strangers,* Zoe thought.

She fixed her attention on the zebra instead. Its mane was short and spiky and it was very fat...in fact, it looked almost like...

Zoe's hands flew to her face in delight as she gasped. "Is that zebra pregnant?"

"Yes," Max said, leading them closer. "We think Candy will give birth in less than a week. That's why she's on her own, away from the other zebras. Once the foal arrives we'll let the two of them bond and then reintroduce them to the herd."

"Wow," Zoe exclaimed. "The Fox family's first zoo baby!"

The zebra keeper, whose name badge read *Jenna*, smiled. "It's a first for Tanglewood too. Baby animals are always a huge hit with the visitors so Candy and her foal will be a real crowd-pleaser, especially now that Tindu isn't arriving for a while."

"Tindu?" Zoe said, frowning.

"Our new Sumatran tiger," her dad explained, looking frustrated. "He's coming from another zoo. We thought he'd be here in time for the reopening but there's a problem with his paperwork."

"The zebras will be the star attraction now," Jenna said. "Although I don't think Candy is happy about being over here by herself. She's a little bored without the others."

"Don't worry, Candy," Zoe said as she stretched her hand over the fence to touch the zebra's black velvet nose. "I'll come and keep you company."

Oliver jerked the brush upwards, knocking Zoe's fingers aside. "Zebras bite," he said sharply. "Don't you know that?"

Zoe felt herself flush with embarrassment. Of course she knew zebras bit sometimes, but Candy had looked so calm that she hadn't thought before she'd reached out. "Sorry."

"Careful, Oliver," Max said, frowning. "You could have hurt Zoe with the brush."

Dad stepped forwards. "It's okay, Max, no harm done. Zoe, you must be more careful. Animals need to get used to you before you start handling them."

Bowing her head, Zoe managed a small nod. She knew her father was right but she wished he hadn't told her off in front of Oliver, who now clearly thought she had no idea how to act around animals. With a silent sigh, she followed Max and her parents away from Candy and Oliver. But her embarrassment soon faded as she and Rory met more of their new neighbors.

A rumbling roar rolled over them as they arrived at Big Cat Mountain.

"That's Sinbad," Max said, "our male African lion. He's letting everyone know this is his territory."

It must have been Sinbad she'd heard back at the house, Zoe realized. She knew lions had the loudest roar of all the big cats and the sound could carry for miles.

"How is Suki's paw?" Mr. Fox asked. "Is it healing?"

Zoe glanced at the information display on the wall. Suki was one of four female lions, recently arrived from a big-cat sanctuary nearby. Two of the other girls were Sinbad's cubs and still young in lion years. The other was fully grown.

"Getting better," Max replied. "She didn't enjoy the journey here much but she seems to be settling in now."

He led them past the lions' den, with its rocky outcrops and wooden platforms, and underneath the bridge that overlooked Big Cat Mountain. Zoe could just see Sinbad's golden mane on one of the flat rocks. She stopped and craned her neck for a better look but at that moment he stood up and stretched. He flicked her a curious look, then stalked away.

"Isn't he amazing?" Zoe said in an awestruck voice. "A real king."

Next they reached the jaguar's home. Zoe shaded her eyes to see if she could see the familiar black and tawny pattern among the leaves and branches but, if the jaguar was there, he was well hidden. Finally, Max and her parents began to slow down.

"Here we are," Max said, pointing at an obviously brand-new enclosure ahead of them. "Snowy Point."

They gazed at the multi-leveled leafy habitat in silence, taking in the enormous boulders and tall trees, and the broad wooden poles that led from one area to another. There were raft-like platforms in front of the glass-fronted tree house so that the public would be able to get up close to the snow leopards while still being protected by thick safety glass. Mrs. Fox pointed out the pipes which harvested rainwater from the eco-friendly roof and carried it to trickle over the rocks into a pool in one corner. In front of where they stood there was a padlocked gate in the wire pen that surrounded the enclosure, which led to a bolted metal door in the wood-and-glass interior fence.

"Wow," said Dad, reaching across to squeeze Mom's hand. "This looks incredible."

"It does," Max agreed. He pulled the keys from his pocket. "Should we see what Minty and Tara think?"

Zoe's mom looked nervous and excited at the same time. "Absolutely."

Max unlocked the padlocked wire gate. Once he and Mr. Fox were both inside, he locked it again and turned his attention to the metal door. They vanished inside.

"Where did Daddy go?" Rory asked.

"He's gone inside to let the snow leopards out," Mom explained. "This is their new home so they'll be very anxious because it won't smell right yet.

I expect Max has some food for them to tempt them out into the open."

Sure enough, a moment later, Max appeared in the enclosure, a lump of meat in his hands. Zoe looked away – she wasn't exactly squeamish but she didn't really like to think about what the leopard food had once been. Max placed the meat on one of the high rocks and then repeated the process with another chunk, this time jamming it between two tree branches so the big cats would need to climb up to get to it. Then he vanished back inside.

The seconds ticked by. Then, after a faint creak, Zoe saw a low metal gate slide up inside the enclosure. She held her breath, unable to believe her luck as a white, whiskery muzzle poked out of the gap and two pale, black-rimmed eyes turned to look at her. The snow leopard studied her warily for a moment then twitched its nose and slunk out of the gate, closely followed by her sister.

Staying close to the ground and sniffing the air, the snow leopards started to explore their new domain, gazing in curiosity at the wooden poles. Zoe had to stop herself from squeaking with excitement when one leaped effortlessly upwards and padded along the narrow beams while the other roamed around the floor, her tail swishing back and forth.

Zoe pulled out her phone and snapped a photo, staring at the silvery soft fur in awe. She'd never been this close to big cats. "I wish I could pet them."

Beside her, Mrs. Fox looked delighted. "They seem to like their new home, don't they?"

Zoe slipped her hand into her mother's and squeezed. "I think they love it, Mom."

Once the adults were happy the snow leopards had settled into Snowy Point, they all made their way back to the manor house. As they passed each enclosure, Zoe tried to figure out which animal it would house – the meerkats' home was sandy, the gibbons and the mischievous chimpanzees needed plenty of room to swing and the penguins had an inviting deep pool.

They trooped back through the front door, Zoe chatting with her parents and Rory yowling and growling like a snow leopard. It wasn't until everyone had picked up their things to go upstairs that Zoe noticed her tiger-striped backpack was missing.

"Where's my bag?"

Her mother frowned. "Is it still in the car?"

"No," Zoe said, shaking her head. "I brought it inside when we arrived. I remember leaving it right here."

"I'm sure it will turn up," Mrs. Fox soothed.

Zoe stared at the wooden floor, feeling perplexed. The bag had been a leaving present from her best friend, Rosalind, and it was too new for her to have grown careless with. She was *sure* she'd had it before they'd gone to see the snow leopards…

Zoe gazed around the hall in confusion. Where could it have gone?

Chapter Three

The next morning, Zoe was awoken by piercing whistles and shouting outside her window. Groaning, she pulled the covers over her head. She was still tired – there were no curtains in her new room, and it had taken her forever to fall asleep. The packing boxes cast strange shadows in the moonlight and her imagination had gone crazy over the creaks and groans of the old building, keeping her awake. Now she'd been woken up by the cheery shouts of the builders putting up the scaffolding so they could repair the roof.

Sitting up, she squinted at the time and was surprised to see it was almost eight o'clock. Her stomach started to rumble. Breakfast first, she decided, then she was going to explore the park.

It took Zoe three attempts to find the kitchen. When she did finally reach it, her mother was already there, sitting at a table which had been too big for their old house but now looked small in this huge room.

"Morning," Zoe called, taking in the clutter.

There were boxes everywhere she looked – on the floor, on the work surfaces, even on the cherry-red stove that sat to the side of the kitchen. Zoe scratched her head, wondering where the cereal was.

Mrs. Fox looked up from her laptop with a smile. "Good morning, sleepyhead. Did the builders wake you?"

Zoe nodded. "Yep. Isn't Rory up yet? Where's Dad?"

Mom made a face. "Rory slept badly so he's still in bed. Dad's been in the park since the crack of dawn, checking on the animals." She smiled again. "He said you could pop over when you're ready. The guinea pigs need cleaning out, apparently."

"No problem," Zoe said. She was looking forward to getting to know all the residents of Tanglewood, from the smallest to the biggest. "Did you or Dad see my backpack anywhere?"

"Sorry," Mrs. Fox said, shaking her head. "We had a good look for it after you'd gone to bed but couldn't find it. I'm sure it'll turn up."

Zoe sighed. "I suppose so," she said and then brightened at the thought of exploring the park. "Any idea where the cereal is? The sooner I eat, the sooner I can go and meet the rest of the animals!"

Zoe slammed the front door behind her and cut through the gate that led into the park. The distant rumble of machinery told her that the builders were hard at work. There was so much to see; she was sure she'd get lost more than once over the coming days but she didn't really mind, not when losing her way meant she might discover a new animal.

A sign on her right pointed to Wolf Woods. She peered into the enclosure and was disappointed to discover that it appeared to be empty. She glanced at her watch – surely she had time for a quick detour? – and took the narrow path that led around the back of the lair, hoping to catch a glimpse of gray fur among the logs and leaves. But there was no sign that anyone was at home.

As Zoe rounded the last corner, she had the strangest feeling she was being watched. It was darker here, and cooler, the path shaded by trees to create the impression that visitors really were in the heart of Wolf Woods. She glanced upwards, scanning the branches that criss-crossed overhead to see if it was a squirrel or a bird that had triggered her sixth sense, but she couldn't see anything. Shrugging, she went on. If she was right, she should come out opposite the picnic area and from there—

The hairs on the back of her neck prickled in warning. Zoe stopped and turned around. She'd definitely heard something this time.

"Who's there?" she called, hoping she didn't sound as nervous as she felt.

No one answered. Birds whistled and sang in the trees. Zoe retraced her steps around the corner and was fast enough to see a flash of something bright vanish around a twist in the trail. Starting to feel uneasy, she decided she'd had enough exploring for now. Hurrying back to the main path, she doubled back towards the guinea pigs.

"What's the matter?" a voice called as she passed the entrance to Wolf Woods again. "Lost already?"

Glancing into the shadows, Zoe saw Oliver leaning against the fence. It must have been him behind her, she realized. Why hadn't he answered her?

"No," she said. "I wanted to see the wolves. Do you know where they are?"

"Of course I do. You can figure it out for yourself, though."

Zoe sighed. Yesterday she'd thought he was shy but now he was being deliberately unhelpful.

"Fine," she said, raising her chin. "I'll ask my dad to show me."

She hadn't gone more than a few steps when Oliver called out again. "You'll never know Tanglewood as well as I do. I've lived here all my life."

Zoe stopped. "I didn't know it was a competition."

"It's not," Oliver said, scowling. "We used to live in the manor house before you came, me and my dad."

Zoe hadn't known the manor had been Max and Oliver's home. She also noticed that he hadn't mentioned his mom. In fact, no one had.

"I'm sorry you had to move out," she said quietly. "Where do you live now?"

Oliver frowned. "In one of the old side cottages." He threw her a disbelieving look. "What do you care, anyway?"

Zoe felt her cheeks going red. "Look—"

"Running Tanglewood isn't going to be easy, you know," he said. "Your parents might know a lot about animals but it's going to take more than a couple of snow leopards to fix things."

Zoe was speechless – that wasn't fair. The park had been closed for months and everywhere she looked work was being done to update things. Her parents had used their zoo contacts all over the country to find new animals to bring in the crowds. They knew plenty about running a successful wildlife park.

Pushing himself away from the fence, Oliver brushed past her. "You'd be better off going back home."

Zoe stared at his retreating back. Oliver seemed determined to dislike her and her family before he even got to know them. Pushing his unpleasantness to the back of her mind, she set off for the guinea pigs again. If Oliver wanted to act like a sulky kid, that was his problem. Zoe had better things to do.

The guinea pigs were all so adorable and fluffy that Zoe soon forgot about Oliver. Some of them were black and white, some were coppery-orange and some were a mixture of all three, but they all had pointy crowns of fur on the top of their heads. A few seemed shy, huddling together in the back of the hutch when she entered their fenced-off run, squeaking loudly like little furry burglar alarms, but most were curious and nosy.

A gold-and-black guinea pig nibbled on Zoe's shoelace.

"That's Digger," said Paolo, their keeper. "She's the nosiest of them all."

Zoe lifted Digger up, peering into her beady black eyes. "Hello."

Digger gazed back at her from underneath her golden bangs and meeped softly. Zoe ruffled the fur on the top of her head and the guinea pig half closed her eyes, as though it was her favorite thing ever.

Paolo laughed. "I think she likes you, or maybe

she just knows you have food in your pocket."

Zoe lowered the guinea pig into the special basket Paolo had given her. "No treats until your house is clean," she said. "So the sooner you all come here, the faster you'll get your tummies filled."

Paolo and Zoe got to work. The guinea-pig enclosure needed to be cleaned out every day, just like all the other animal pens at Tanglewood. They replaced the dirty sawdust and straw from the floor and inside the wooden hutches, swept up any half-chewed food and refilled the water bottles. Finally they put down fresh vegetables and hay, then let the guinea pigs out.

"Great work," Paolo said, smiling, as they made a beeline for the cabbage and carrot tops. "We could use another pair of hands around here; it's just me and the other keeper, Fern, most days, so we're a bit stretched. How would you feel about joining Team GP on a regular basis?"

"Really?" Zoe gasped. "Oh, I'd love to!"

Paolo looked pleased. "Great. I'll talk to your dad

about adding you to the cleaning and feeding schedule."

"That would be fantastic," Zoe said, beaming.

One of her dreams was to be a keeper when she was older – joining Team GP would be a great way to get some hands-on animal experience.

"Those look like very happy piggies," a voice said behind them.

Zoe turned around to see a short, dark-haired woman smiling at her.

"Hello, Zoe," the woman said. "I'm Mizbah, the lemur keeper. I hear you're a big lemur fan."

"Definitely," Zoe replied. "I love them, especially the ring-tails. How many do you have?"

"Ten," Mizbah said. "I can introduce you to them if you like? What are you up to this afternoon?"

Zoe tried not to groan. "Unpacking boxes," she said, making a face. "Mom says the sooner we get them out of the way, the better."

"Sounds sensible. Tomorrow, then?" Mizbah

offered. "Eight thirty? You can help me to give them their breakfast."

"I'd like that," Zoe said, feeling a bubble of happiness grow inside her.

Life at Tanglewood was turning out to be every bit as fur-filled as she'd hoped it would be.

🦏

"I'm sure there weren't this many boxes when we packed the house," Zoe's mother said, as they opened up what felt like the hundredth container marked "Kitchen" and began to unpack it. "It's never-ending."

It was just after lunch. Rory must have been more exhausted by the move than anyone had realized because he'd dozed off almost before he'd finished eating and was now upstairs having a nap. Zoe could hear the buzz of the old baby monitor her mom had dug out so that she could get on with some unpacking while Rory slept in his room. They hadn't needed it at their old house but the manor was so much bigger.

Zoe had been amazed to find Rory in the yard

with Oliver when she'd gotten back from Guinea Pig Central, the two of them watching a slug glide across the grass with fascinated expressions. She supposed Oliver was embarrassed about the way he'd acted earlier, because he'd vanished into the woods before she got too close.

"Did you see Oliver on your travels around the park?" Mom asked, lifting out some dinner plates and carrying them to the cabinet.

"Here and there," Zoe said, trying not to grimace.

"Good," Mom said. "Max thinks he's a little lonely. Things haven't been easy since they lost Oliver's mother a few years ago—"

Zoe's head jolted up. *So that's why Oliver hadn't mentioned his mom*, she thought, and felt a stab of sympathy for both Max and Oliver. She couldn't imagine how hard it must be to lose someone you loved.

"Anyway," Mom went on, "it would be great if you could try to make friends with him."

Zoe thought back to earlier. "I'll try," she said,

"but I'm not sure he wants to be friends."

"Give him a chance," Mom said. "He might surprise you."

The back door creaked open and Dad came in. "How's the unpacking going?"

"Slowly," said Zoe and her mother at exactly the same time. They grinned at each other.

"Well, I've got good news and bad news for you, Zoe," her father said and she noticed he was hiding something behind his back. "Which do you want first?"

Mrs. Fox wrinkled her nose. "What is that smell?" She glanced suspiciously down at Mr. Fox's feet. "Have you stepped in something?"

"That's the bad news," Mr. Fox said and he held out his hands, which were clad in rubber gloves. In them was Zoe's tiger-print backpack. It was crusted in mud and smelled awful. "One of the assistant keepers found this on the dung heap."

Zoe pinched her nose. "By bag! How did it get dere?"

"I have absolutely no idea," her dad said. "It was buried pretty deep. You're lucky we decided to move the dung today or we might not have found it for a week."

Mrs. Fox fanned the air in front of her face. "Yuck. Sorry, Zoe, but you can't keep it. You'll have to empty it out and throw it away."

Zoe's heart sank. "But it was a present from Rosalind," she protested. "Can't we put it in the washing machine?"

"I'm afraid not," her mom said. "We'll get you a new one, I promise. Now take it outside and empty it."

Sighing, Zoe snapped on a pair of rubber gloves. Then she took the bag and went outside. There wasn't much inside – a notebook, some pens, and a zebra key ring – but she rescued what she could. With a heavy heart, she lifted the lid of the bin and dropped the dirty backpack inside, with the rubber gloves on top.

"Bye-bye, tiger bag," she said.

"Wash your hands before you touch anything,"

Mrs. Fox instructed the moment Zoe walked back into the kitchen, pointing to the bottle of antibacterial soap by the kitchen sink.

Zoe didn't argue, even though her hands had been protected by the gloves. She knew only too well what nasty diseases could be picked up around animals – germs that wouldn't affect them but could make people very sick. Anyone who spent time in a zoo was used to scrubbing up with germ-killing sprays and soaps.

She was drying her hands when a sudden piercing scream filled the air. All three of them stared at each other in shock as another scream rang out, and another.

"Mommy, Mommy, Mommy! There's a ghost in my room!"

Chapter Four

Mom ran for the stairs, Zoe and her dad right behind her. All three of them burst into Rory's room and found him curled up in a little ball on the bed, sobbing in terror.

Mrs. Fox hurried forwards and gathered him in her arms, holding him close and rubbing his back as she soothed him.

"Shhh, it's okay. We're here now."

"Did you have a bad dream?" Zoe asked.

Rory shook his head, his face white with fear.

"There's a ghost in the walls," he blurted out. "I heard it."

Everyone froze, listening hard, but there was no sound other than Rory's ragged breathing.

"Are you sure it wasn't a dream?" Zoe said.

"Yes!" Rory shouted, his eyes shining with tears as he pointed at the wall. "The ghost is in there and it's going to get me."

Zoe saw her parents exchange looks over her little brother's head.

"Okay," Mrs. Fox said. "Why don't we go downstairs and get a glass of milk? You can tell us all about it."

Clinging to his mother, Rory nodded and Mrs. Fox hoisted him into her arms. Zoe waited until her dad had followed and stood very still in the middle of Rory's room, listening carefully. She heard nothing. Whatever it was that had frightened him, it wasn't there now.

Zoe groaned when her alarm beeped at seven thirty the next morning. She'd gone to bed early, anxious to get a good night's sleep so that she would be fresh to meet the lemurs, but Rory had woken up three times in the night, screaming about ghosts and crying inconsolably. Eventually, their bleary-eyed parents had taken him into bed with them so that they could all get some sleep but Zoe still felt as though someone had sprinkled sand underneath her eyelids when she hit the alarm. Wiggling further under the covers, she let her eyes drift shut for a few more minutes.

She woke up again at 8:18 and let out a cry of horror when she saw the time. She was going to be late! As fast as she could, Zoe pulled on some clothes and tugged the hairbrush through her hair. Then she hurried downstairs, hoping she wouldn't get lost again. She wanted to make a good impression on everyone at Tanglewood and especially on the keepers – the last thing she needed was for Mizbah to think she'd forgotten and start the lemur feed without her.

Mom smiled wearily at Zoe as she huffed into the room. "Good morning. Want some breakfast?"

"No time," Zoe muttered, grabbing the unwanted crusts from Rory's plate. "I'm supposed to be outside the lemur enclosure right now."

Mom's hands flew to her face. "Oh, I completely forgot. Sorry, Zoe, I should have woken you up."

Zoe pulled on her rubber boots. "It's okay. I don't suppose you got much sleep with Mr. Wigglepants over there taking up all the room."

It was a family joke that Rory slept like a starfish with his arms and legs spread out – and a very wiggly starfish at that. But he didn't smile at the new nickname she'd given him. He didn't even look up.

"Hey," Zoe said, ruffling his hair. "Want to come and meet the guinea pigs later?"

"Okay," he replied in a dull voice, as though it was really the last thing he felt like doing.

Zoe frowned – it was very unlike Rory to be disinterested in animals. He must be even more tired than she was. But she didn't have time to worry about it now, she thought with a glance at the clock – she had less than a minute to get to the lemurs.

"Got to go!" she gasped, running to the back door. "Cheer up, Rory, see you later. Bye, Mom!"

Mizbah was waiting outside the ring-tailed lemur habitat, two silver bowls filled with raw fruit and vegetables piled one on top of the other.

"Sorry!" Zoe puffed as she ran along the path. "I'm so sorry I'm late."

Mizbah smiled. "Don't worry, it's fine. I bumped into your dad this morning and he told me all about your sleepless night. He thought you might be a little delayed."

"Oh," Zoe said, wondering why her dad hadn't simply woken her up when he'd left. Then again, he'd probably been up and out of the manor house at dawn, too early for Zoe. "Sorry."

"Stop saying sorry," Mizbah laughed and she held out one of the bowls. "Here, take this."

Zoe took the bowl, studying the mixture of foods. She saw sweet potato, melon, carrots and parsnips, among other things – almost exactly the same as the fruit and vegetables given to the lemurs at the zoo back home.

"Come and meet the gang," Mizbah said as she led Zoe towards the padlocked entrance.

There were two gates, an outer one and an inner one, and both had chunky padlocks on their bolts. The space in between the two gates left enough room for the two of them to stand next to each other but not much more. Zoe watched as Mizbah carefully locked the first gate before she opened the second. "All of our gates have safety locks and we always make sure the outer gate is locked before we open the inner one," Mizbah explained. "But I'm sure you know that already."

Zoe nodded. It had been exactly the same when she'd visited her dad's old work, and she knew that it made sure the animals stayed safe. Once they were inside the inner gate, Mizbah shut that too.

"Now," she said, turning to Zoe, "let's introduce you."

The lemurs were fidgeting beside the gate, watching the humans with their big amber eyes. In some ways, they reminded her of cats – their wavy striped tails and graceful movements were a little bit feline, although their hands were more like hers than an animal's paws.

The breath caught in Zoe's throat as the little creatures sped along the ropes hung from the ceiling – they were so fast, swinging like acrobats around the enclosure. It was incredible being this close. She could almost reach out and touch them.

Mizbah scattered some of the food onto the floor and the lemurs hurried to investigate. The keeper pointed at each gray head.

"There's Stripe and Gizmo and Georgie. The one with the banana is Milo."

One of the animals leaped up Zoe's body and settled on her shoulder, peering nosily down at the bowl she held, making her laugh in delight.

"And your new best friend is Bindi. She's the mother of the group and the one who's in charge."

Zoe held out a lump of carrot and Bindi leaned down to examine it. Then she reached past Zoe's hand and plucked a cube of melon from the dish. Mizbah laughed.

"Bindi's got a terrible sweet tooth. Offer her fruit and she'll be your friend forever."

A friend was exactly what she needed, Zoe thought, admiring Bindi's delicate fingers as she nibbled at the melon. The lemur's gaze darted around the enclosure as though she expected someone to snatch it from her at any moment. The others were too busy investigating the food on the floor, however, and they didn't give Zoe much more than a curious look.

She stroked the black-and-white tail curled around her neck, ruffling the soft fur. If only there was a way to make friends with Oliver. Now that she'd had time to think about it, Zoe understood why he'd been so prickly – if she'd had to give up her home to make room for strangers, she'd be upset too.

With all the changes, it must feel like they were taking over everything. He reminded her of Sinbad the lion, roaring to mark his territory – all she had to do was make him understand she wasn't a threat.

"Have you met Candy yet?" Mizbah asked. "We've been lucky enough to have quite a few lemurs born at Tanglewood in the past but we're all looking forward to having a baby zebra."

Zoe felt a little fizz of joy. "I saw her when we arrived. Max said the foal is due in less than a week."

"It is," Mizbah said. "I think Candy will be glad once it's all over and not just because she'll have a gorgeous baby to look after. It's no fun for her being in isolation; she misses the herd."

That was what Jenna had said too, Zoe thought as she stroked Bindi's furry tummy. Maybe she'd stop by Candy's enclosure once she'd finished with the lemurs. From the sounds of things, the zebra needed a friend too.

Zoe's stomach had begun to rumble loudly long before she'd finished helping Mizbah with the lemurs, so she decided to grab some breakfast before heading over to see Candy. But when she got home, she found her mother was struggling with a very clingy and tearful Rory while trying to answer the phone and work on her laptop at the same time. From the looks of things, Mrs. Fox wasn't managing any of it successfully.

"Rory, I can't see the screen. Please stop pressing the buttons. We can play cards in a minute!" She threw Zoe a harassed look and puffed a stray lock of hair out of her eyes. "He's been like this all morning. I'm supposed to have finished this report on the plants for the new meerkat house by lunchtime so the site manager can order them. At this rate it'll be *tomorrow* lunchtime before it's done."

Zoe grabbed a banana. "Mmm," she said, chewing on a mouthful. "Ngggh."

A handful of animal matching cards were scattered on the floor under the table. Picking them up, Zoe added them to the rest of the pack and started to shuffle them, smiling when she saw the zebra card. She couldn't wait to see Candy.

Mrs. Fox fired a hopeful look Zoe's way. "I don't suppose you'd play with Rory for a while, would you? So I can finish my report?"

"But I've got things to do," Zoe objected, seeing her plans melt away. "Can't Dad come back and watch him?"

"No, he's busy with the monkey vaccinations," her mother said, sighing. "Please, Zoe, I really need to get this done."

Zoe looked at Rory's tight, miserable expression. *He wasn't normally like this*, she thought. It must be because he was tired. But she was tired too and she'd set her heart on visiting Candy. She couldn't do that with Rory – the last thing a pregnant zebra needed was a tantrum-throwing little boy disturbing her peace and quiet. Then she glanced up at her mother's red face and realized how stressed she was. Candy was going to have to wait.

"Okay," she grumbled. "Just this once."

"Thanks, darling," Mrs. Fox said. "Maybe you could head over to the cafe? There's a soft-play area that I'm sure Rory would love."

The cafe wasn't as empty as Zoe had expected. Builders were dotted around the silver tables and big squashy sofas, wearing hard hats and drinking coffee. A rosy-cheeked woman was standing behind the counter next to the entrance, keeping everyone supplied with drinks and snacks. She beamed at Zoe and Rory as they came in.

"Hello. I'm Dolly, the catering manager."

"Nice to meet you," Zoe said and introduced herself and her brother. "Rory's come to play, if that's okay?"

"Perfectly okay," Dolly said, waving her hand at the brightly colored structure of padded stairs and tunnels. "Oliver is in there already."

Zoe remembered her mom's suggestion that she make friends with Oliver.

"Great," she said to Dolly, with a smile. "Come

on, Rory, let's see if we can find him."

She kicked off her shoes and followed Rory into the maze of tunnels. But even though they explored every nook and cranny, they didn't find Oliver.

"Let's get a drink," Zoe suggested eventually, after chasing Rory through the ball pit for the tenth time.

They sat at one of the cafe tables. Dolly brought them tall glasses of ice-cold lemonade.

"I thought you might like this," she said, holding out an old map of the park. "It's changed a bit but it might help you find your way around."

Rory immediately began to pore over the map and Zoe gave Dolly a grateful smile.

"Look, there are the lions," Rory said, pointing at the pictures. "And the gibbons and the meerkats and the penguins."

Zoe nodded. There was so much to see at Tanglewood. As her brother chattered non-stop about which animals he wanted to see most, Zoe gazed around. She was about to suggest to Rory that they went to explore the park when she heard a faint rustling sound. A torn candy wrapper drifted down from above and landed on the table.

Rory didn't notice. Zoe stared upwards and spotted a sock-covered foot poking out from a hidden cubbyhole she hadn't noticed before. *So that was where Oliver was*, she thought. He was hiding directly above them, eavesdropping on their conversation! She frowned. There had to be a way to get him to join in…

She glanced at the map and an idea popped into her head. Oliver thought he knew everything about Tanglewood. If she made a mistake about an animal she bet he wouldn't be able to resist correcting her.

"See the red pandas, Rory?" she said, clearing her throat. "They live in South America and they eat—"

Oliver's head appeared above them.

"No, they don't," he interrupted. "They're from the East Himalayas, everyone knows that."

Zoe pretended to frown. "If you know so much about them, why don't you prove it?"

"All right," he said, scrambling out of the

cubbyhole and into the maze of tunnels.

A moment later, he arrived beside their table.

"They live in trees and mostly eat bamboo, although they like fruit and insects too. Their natural habitat is under threat from deforestation so they're a vulnerable species. And they're nowhere near as big or as famous as giant pandas. They're bigger than a cat but smaller than a lot of dogs."

"They also eat birds' eggs," Rory piped up. "And sometimes lizards."

"That's right," Oliver said, staring at him in obvious surprise. He fired a contemptuous look at Zoe. "At least one of you knows what you're talking about."

Zoe pressed her lips together and said nothing. Oliver seemed determined to be mean – now she wished she hadn't bothered trying to include him.

"Anyway, I've got better things to do than hang around with losers," Oliver went on, bending down to pull his shoes out from underneath a nearby sofa. He tugged them on and slouched to the exit.

Dolly watched him go and then bustled over to

Zoe and Rory. "I don't know what's gotten into him, he's normally such a nice boy," she said.

It's me, Zoe realized. *He likes Rory just fine, it's me he doesn't like.* She summoned up a smile for Dolly and nodded.

"I'm sure he'll get used to us being around soon." She glanced at the big clock on the wall, then at Rory. "Mom will have finished her report by now. Do you need a nap?"

His expression changed like lightning.

"No," he said, shaking his head violently from side to side. "I'm not tired."

He was, Zoe decided, taking in his glassy stare and heavy eyelids, but she wasn't going to argue.

"Okay," she said. "Do you want to come and check on the guinea pigs with me?"

"Yes," Rory said. "But no sleep. Not until the ghost goes away."

They waved goodbye to Dolly and headed to the guinea-pig pen. Zoe went inside, giving Rory strict instructions to wait at the gate while she checked their food and water. Digger scurried over immediately, obviously hoping Zoe had some more snacks in her pockets. Zoe picked the little animal up, laughing.

"No treats today, girl. Here, Rory, meet Digger."

Rory reached out and carefully stroked the guinea pig's back. "Hello, Digger."

Digger squeaked a friendly greeting and Zoe lowered her to the ground. She was just about to leave the enclosure, satisfied everything was clean and neat, when she noticed a gray-and-white bundle huddled in one corner. Frowning, she made her way towards it and saw it was a young guinea pig named Fluff. She kneeled down, stroking the animal's trembling body. Fluff meeped shrilly at her touch and she saw his leg was bent at a funny angle.

"Oh," she exclaimed in dismay, "have you hurt yourself?"

She leaned down to inspect the leg more closely, being careful not to touch it. The guinea pig squeaked miserably and Zoe gasped in sympathy. His leg was horribly twisted – the poor little creature must be in agony. She straightened up, filled with concern. The damage to the leg was awful – it looked broken. But whether it was broken or not, one thing was clear: Fluff needed urgent medical attention. Small animals like guinea pigs could die from the shock and pain of an injury like this. Time was running out.

"Come on," she said, trying not to panic as she picked her way back to Rory. "Fluff needs help and he needs it now!"

Chapter Five

Zoe sped along the path, her stomach churning with worry for poor Fluff. Where were all the keepers? She didn't care who she found as long as they could help the stricken guinea pig.

She almost sobbed with relief when Rory spotted a figure in the distance.

"Come on," she urged her little brother, breaking into a run. "Excuse me! Stop, please!"

The figure turned around. Zoe groaned when she

saw that it was Oliver. Of all the people it could have been, why did it have to be him? But there was no time to find anyone else; Fluff's life depended on quick treatment.

"Oliver!" she called. "Wait!"

He started to walk away. Gritting her teeth, Zoe started to run again.

"Come on, Rory. Let's pretend to be cheetahs."

Oliver didn't even look at her when they caught up with him.

"What do you want?" he snapped.

Zoe didn't waste any time.

"Fluff the guinea pig is injured," she panted. "He needs help."

Oliver stopped. His eyes narrowed. "I knew it – you've got no idea how to handle animals. What did you do to Fluff?"

She gaped at the unfairness of the accusation. "I didn't do anything! His leg looks broken but it was like that when we found him."

"Then what happened?"

Zoe huffed in frustration. "I don't know. We don't have time to argue about this now, I'm scared Fluff is going to die."

His face paled and she knew she'd convinced him.

"Okay," he said. "Dad was with the alpacas five minutes ago. If you're quick you should catch him."

She glanced down at the phone in his hand. "Can't you call him? Or any of the other keepers? I could meet them at the guinea-pig enclosure."

"Battery's dead," he said, looking a little embarrassed. "I spent too long on it. You'd better run."

"Right," Zoe said, then hesitated. "Where are the alpacas?"

Oliver snorted. "You really don't know anything, do you?"

"I know lots of things," she replied, trying to keep her temper. "But I don't know my way around every bit of the park yet and we left the map in the cafe. This is important – please would you show us?"

For a heartbeat she thought he would refuse.

Then he jerked his head to one side. "This way."

They hurried along in silence. Rory's shorter legs slowed them down – he did his best to keep up but he was already tired and starting to complain. Oliver glanced at Rory and Zoe. "I'll run ahead and tell Dad what's happened," he said, speeding up.

"Wait!" Zoe cried as he ran off, but Oliver didn't seem to hear.

Biting her lip, Zoe did her best to coax her brother along. Max and Oliver were in the alpaca enclosure when Zoe and Rory arrived. Zoe waited at the gate, trying to control her impatience but it was hard whenever she pictured Fluff lying there in pain. She saw Oliver point back the way they'd come and gesture urgently. His voice was too low for Zoe to catch. Then the direction of the breeze changed and she suddenly heard more clearly. "...don't know what she did but legs don't break themselves."

Max raised his head and stared at Zoe, before striding over.

"What happened?" the vet asked. "Oliver says

one of the guinea pigs is hurt."

Pushing her anxiety about what Oliver had told his father aside, Zoe explained about Fluff's leg. When she finished, Max looked worried.

"I need to get over there right away. A broken leg is really bad news for a guinea pig."

"I know," Zoe said, biting her lip. She hoped they weren't too late.

Fluff barely moved when they opened the gate. Oliver waited with Rory while Max and Zoe went inside. The vet's expression was serious as he lifted the injured animal and examined him. Zoe felt her eyes fill with tears as Fluff squeaked in pain. Broken legs weren't always treatable and she wouldn't be able to bear it if Max said the kindest thing would be to put the guinea pig out of its misery.

"How did it happen?" Max asked.

"I don't know," Zoe said. "They were all fine when we cleaned their pen out yesterday. Rory and I stopped by on our way back from the cafe and found Fluff hiding in the corner."

Max glanced over at Oliver, then turned his gaze back to Zoe.

"You're sure he was already like this? Accidents do happen and I know guinea pigs can be hard to hold if you're not used to them."

Zoe felt her cheeks grow hot with embarrassment. Did Max really think she didn't know how to handle animals? She glanced over at Oliver, who looked away. Her eyes narrowed.

"I *am* used to them," she said. That was what he'd meant by "legs don't break themselves" – he was suggesting *she'd* hurt Fluff. She couldn't bear that Max thought she was no good with animals. He might stop her from being part of Team GP, or worse, from helping with *any* of Tanglewood's residents.

She turned an anxious gaze back to the vet, determined to convince him she was innocent.

"I don't know how Fluff hurt his leg but it wasn't anything to do with Rory or me."

Max held her gaze for a moment longer then nodded.

"It's a good thing you found him when you did." Cradling Fluff against his chest, he lifted his radio to his mouth. "Calling Libby in the medical center?"

The radio crackled and burst into life. "Libby here. What's up?"

"We need urgent support at the guinea-pig enclosure," he said, his voice terse. "Bring a straw-lined box for transport."

When Max had finished on the radio, he reached into his bag and withdrew a small syringe in a sterile plastic bag, and a tiny bottle.

"This is for the pain," he told Zoe. "Once we get Fluff back to the medical center, I can take a closer look at that leg and decide what to do next."

Zoe swallowed hard. "He's...he's not going to die, is he?"

"Not if I can help it," Max said, his mouth twisting into a smile. "Now, do you think you can hold Fluff steady while I give him an injection?"

Zoe nodded, taking the trembling animal and holding him with tender hands while Max filled the syringe and inserted it into the scruff of Fluff's neck. He massaged the fur gently once he was done. "There. That should start to take effect right away."

Fluff's squeaks began to die down and he lay still and quiet in Zoe's arms until Libby the nurse arrived with the box. Together, they nestled the guinea pig into the straw, taking care not to move his damaged leg. Zoe touched his head once before the box was closed.

"Bye, Fluff," she said in a subdued voice. "I'll come and visit you soon."

"Try not to worry," Max said. "He's a strong little thing. With some luck it will be a clean break and he'll be scampering around like normal very soon."

Max and Libby headed off, leaving Zoe, Oliver and Rory staring after them. An awkward silence filled the air. Zoe wanted to ask Oliver what he'd told his dad about Fluff's injury, whether he'd meant to make it sound like it was her fault. Because if he had—

"There you are!" Zoe's mother cried, coming along the path towards them.

"Mommy!" Rory said, and ran to hug her.

Mrs. Fox swept him into her arms. "I heard what happened. How's Fluff?"

Zoe explained, leaving out what she'd heard Oliver tell Max for now. When she'd finished, Mom looked concerned.

"It sounds like you've all had a difficult time. Why don't you come back to the manor for some lunch? You too, Oliver, I'm sure I can rustle something up for you."

Zoe let out a hiss of annoyance. The last thing she wanted was to have to look at him while she ate her lunch. "I think Oliver's busy," she said.

Was it her imagination or did he almost smirk?

"No I'm not," he said. "Thank you, Mrs. Fox, I'd love some lunch."

Zoe's mother beamed. "Great. I just need to run over to Snowy Point. I'll meet you back at the house."

Oliver waited until Mrs. Fox had gone before

flashing a triumphant look at Zoe, and she knew he'd only said yes to annoy her. She fired a resentful glare his way and hung back, trailing along behind in irritated silence. Oliver and Rory chattered about the animals they were passing, sharing fact after fact. Zoe didn't join in, not even when she was burning to prove she wasn't as clueless as Oliver thought.

As they reached the gate to the manor house, Rory slowed down and looked up at Oliver.

"I heard the ghost," he said, his voice small and worried. "It was inside the wall, just like you said it would be."

Zoe stared at Oliver. "What does he mean, 'just like you said it would be'?"

Oliver's cheeks turned red. "How should I know?" he said. "He's just a little kid, they talk nonsense."

"I'm not talking nonsense," Rory said, his face squinted up in sudden fury. "You said the manor was haunted by a ghost. You said he lived in the walls and I know he's there because I heard him too, but Zoe says she won't let him get me."

Oliver's expression was a mixture of surprise and guilt. "Get real. Everyone knows there's no such thing."

But his eyes were shifty as he looked away and Zoe knew he was lying. She felt a surge of anger.

"You?" she said, her voice shaking. "You told him that? Why?"

"Calm down," Oliver muttered. "He asked me about the house so I told him an old story. I didn't make it up – everyone knows it. Just like they know that it's really the—"

"He's only four years old!" Zoe snapped, feeling her blood boil with anger. "How could you be so stupid? He was too scared to sleep last night – you gave him nightmares."

Oliver looked uneasy, as though he knew he'd been caught in the wrong.

"Tell him you lied," Zoe demanded. "Ghosts aren't real. The dead stay dead."

Oliver took a step back, his face suddenly gray. Too late, Zoe realized what she'd said and how it must have sounded to Oliver. Horrified, she clamped her hand over her mouth. But Oliver had already turned on his heel and gone back into the park. Zoe felt sick at her own stupidity – she'd forgotten his mother was dead. Beside her, Rory started to cry.

As quick as a flash, Zoe kneeled down beside him.

"Don't listen, Rory. Oliver is just – well, you heard him. There's no such thing as ghosts."

Her brother sniffed. "I want to go back to our old house. There were no ghosts there."

Zoe took his hand. "There aren't any here, either, just lots and lots of nice animals."

His lip wobbled, as though he didn't quite believe her. Zoe gave him a reassuring smile.

"I'll tell you what, if you promise to forget about all that I could take you up to see Candy after lunch."

He nodded, looking a tiny bit happier. Zoe led him back to the house, trying to calm her jangling temper. She wished she could go back in time and tell herself not to be so thoughtless with Oliver.

Or maybe even further so she could stop Fluff from being hurt, except that she had no idea when his injury had happened.

It was so unfair of Oliver to try and blame her for that – now that she'd seen how sneaky he'd been with Rory she was sure he'd lied to his father about Fluff. She ought to tell her parents what a bully Oliver was being, although she didn't know what they'd do – speak to Max, probably.

One thing she was sure of, she decided as she stomped into the house, she wasn't going to bother trying to make friends with Oliver any more. It was clear she was wasting her time.

Chapter Six

Zoe woke suddenly in the night.

She wasn't sure at first what had woken her – the bedroom was silent, the curtains drawn to keep the moonlight from waking her up. She listened hard, hoping to hear whatever it was that Rory could hear inside the walls. It didn't matter how many times Zoe and her parents told him there was no such thing as ghosts, he insisted there was something there. And then she heard it – a faint scritching-scratching sound from somewhere behind her head.

She froze, hardly daring to breathe. The scratching was followed by the creak of floorboards in the hallway outside and a squeak as her door handle turned. The door sighed open. Zoe pulled the covers up to her chin, her heart racing.

"Zoe?" her dad whispered, framed in the light from the hall. "Are you awake?"

"Dad, you scared me!" Zoe grumbled, letting out the breath she'd been holding in a whoosh. "What are you doing?"

He flicked the light switch, filling the room with brightness. All thoughts of the mysterious noise vanished when she saw he was fully dressed. "What—?"

"Candy is about to have her foal," he said. "I wondered if you might like to come and watch?"

Zoe sat straight up in bed. She felt as though all her Christmases and birthdays had come at once.

"Can I? Oh please, can I?"

Her dad let out a low laugh. "I'll take that as a yes, then. Get dressed and I'll meet you in the kitchen in five minutes."

It took Zoe three attempts to get her sweatshirt on the right way. She'd never seen an animal being born before, and this was the first baby to be born since they'd moved in the park. Her stomach fizzed with anticipation and she could hardly breathe from the excitement.

"You'll have to be whisper-quiet," her dad warned as they made their way through the cool night to the barn. "Even the slightest sound might scare Candy and I don't want to stop her labor. It would be dangerous for both her and the foal."

Zoe nodded and pretended to zip her lips. "I understand."

"Max is already there," he went on. "From what he's said, I don't think it will be long before the foal makes an appearance. We'll let Candy get on with things as much as possible and only help if we need to."

Hurrying along beside him, Zoe resisted the urge to skip with happiness. She had to be calm and show her dad she could be quiet and sensible, then maybe he'd let her be there for other animal births. Imagine if she got to see a ring-tailed lemur being born!

The stable was warm and bright. Candy was lying on her side on the hay, her tummy round and her sides heaving as she huffed and puffed. Every now and then, she got up and peered around at her stomach, as though wondering what was going on. Zoe recognized Jenna, the keeper in charge of the zebras, standing beside Max. Both were watching Candy with anxious eyes. And next to them was Oliver.

Zoe couldn't help it – she groaned. Oliver was the last person she wanted to see and he didn't look pleased to see her either. It had been two days since she'd confronted him about the ghost story and she had done her best to avoid him since then. Not only was she still angry, but she also cringed every time she remembered what she'd blurted out in the heat of the argument. This definitely wasn't the time for another showdown, though, so she hid her dismay in a big yawn and resolved to stay on her side of the barn.

"Wait here," her father said in a soft voice, pointing to a hay bale. "And remember, be quiet."

Zoe sat down and her father made his way carefully around to Max and Jenna. They began to talk in hushed voices and a moment later, a sullen-faced Oliver started to walk towards Zoe. He slumped onto the hay bale, ignoring her. She edged as far away as she could manage, fixing her eyes on Candy. She wouldn't let him spoil this for her, she *wouldn't*.

Candy let out a soft whinny and lowered herself to the straw again. Briefly, her head rested on the ground, as though she was taking a nap, and then she twisted around to stare at her tail. With another gentle nicker, she rolled almost onto her back, all four legs in the air. Max and Jenna and Mr. Fox stopped their whispered conversation to watch. Zoe nibbled her nails in nervous fascination as a white bubble – the sac – appeared at the back of the zebra. Could that be…? Candy's sides heaved and her legs jerked as more of the bubble was squeezed out. Zoe leaned forward. She could just about make out a dark shape inside the bubble. Eyes wide, she held her breath. Beside her, Oliver moved forwards too.

"Look," she murmured. "Is that the head?"

All of a sudden, Candy lurched to her feet. Zoe froze, scared she had frightened the zebra, but after a few restless circles, Candy settled back down on the straw in exactly the same position she'd been in before and her sides began to heave again. The bubble grew larger and now Zoe was sure she could see the foal's head, although it was still inside the sac. Long minutes passed and everyone waited. Little by little, more of the foal appeared. Zoe felt her excitement growing – soon there would be a brand-new baby zebra next to Candy. Oliver was glued to the scene as well, looking every bit as thrilled as Zoe felt.

And then just as suddenly as it had begun, everything seemed to stop. The bubble didn't get any bigger and Candy took longer and longer breaks in between pushes, her head lying flat against the straw. *She's running out of strength*, Zoe thought, and her gaze flew to her father. Max, Jenna and Dad were deep in conversation, their expressions grave. Then Max kneeled by Candy and eased the white bubble apart, revealing a long, narrow nose. Zoe saw Jenna crouch by Candy's head. She murmured encouragement to the zebra and after a few seconds, her legs began to twitch again. Relief whooshed through Zoe as more of the foal slithered into view.

"Not fast enough," mumbled Oliver, looking anxious. "The foal's in trouble."

Zoe's head whipped around. "How do you know?"

"I've seen it before," he whispered back. "If a foal takes too long to be born, it might die." His troubled gaze flickered back to Candy. "They both might."

He lapsed into silence. Zoe twisted her hands

in her lap, trying to stay calm. Surely they wouldn't let Candy and her foal die?

Candy let out a high-pitched whinny and Oliver leaned forward again. "They're going to have to help."

Sure enough, Zoe saw Max's gloved hands ease behind the foal's head and begin to gently pull on the animal's shoulders. Candy's legs began to jerk harder as her foal slid and slithered into the world. And then, with one final push, it was all over. The last of the white bubble slipped onto the straw and with it came the foal.

Candy lay still, breathing hard as Max cleared the sac from the foal's mouth and nose with careful hands. He rubbed the little striped body with a clean towel, drying and massaging at the same time. Zoe held her breath. Was the foal moving? It was so hard to tell…

The little head jerked. Zoe gasped with relief as it began to wiggle and twitch. Next to her, Oliver punched the air and she saw her father exchange thankful looks with Max and Jenna. Candy raised her head and twisted around to nuzzle her newborn.

"Oh!" Zoe said, as the foal lifted a wobbly nose to meet its mother. "They're so gorgeous together."

Max cleared the remains of the birth sac away and sat back.

"We just need to wait for the umbilical cord to break and then we can leave them alone for some mother-and-baby time."

"Amazing," Zoe sighed, watching the foal wiggle around on the straw.

Candy turned her head again and began to lick the foal's cheek.

"Although I'm glad my mom doesn't do that to me."

Oliver nodded. "Yeah."

Something about the way he said it made Zoe wonder if he was thinking about his own mother again.

"I – I'm sorry about what I said the other day. I didn't mean to upset you."

He stiffened. "It's okay. You didn't really."

Zoe hesitated. She wasn't sure she believed him. "Oh. Well, I'm still sorry."

They sat in silence until Max picked up a spray can. "This is iodine, for the end of the cord."

He sprayed underneath the foal for a few seconds, then stood up.

"And that's it. Welcome to the world, little one. I hope you're ready to be a superstar because you're going to be a smash hit with our visitors."

"Is it a boy or a girl?" Zoe asked, as the foal tried to climb onto its spindly legs and failed. It looked so cute and wobbly and *adorable* – she longed to go and help but she knew her dad wouldn't let her. The foal had to learn to stand up on its own or it wouldn't be able to get milk from Candy.

"A boy," Mr. Fox said. "Actually, Jenna and I were just wondering whether you and Oliver could think of a name for him."

"You were?" Zoe exclaimed, feeling as though she might burst with delight. "I'd love that!"

Oliver straightened up. "How about Flash?"

Zoe's smile faded. "I was thinking of Ziggy."

"Um, no," Oliver said, his lip curling. "Not happening."

"What's wrong with Ziggy?" Zoe fired back. "His stripes even look a little like zigzags."

Oliver rolled his eyes. "It's a stupid name."

Zoe's dad lifted a hand. "If you two can't agree, we'll let Rory name the foal," he said, his tone stern. "So what's it going to be?"

Zoe felt Oliver's eyes boring into her. She really liked the name she'd suggested – the foal looked like a Ziggy and after the way Oliver had treated Rory she didn't feel like giving in to him about anything. But then she remembered how she'd made friends with Bindi the lemur by giving her some melon. Maybe the foal's name was something she could give to Oliver, to show him she wasn't there to make his life harder. Maybe…

"Okay," she said, hoping she didn't sound as grudging as she felt. "We can call him Flash if you want."

A look of surprise crossed Oliver's face, followed by one of triumph. "All right!" he whooped and held up a hand. "High five!"

Zoe hesitated, then smacked her palm against his before he could whisk it away and make her look like a fool. "High five for Flash the zebra!" she said with a smile.

Chapter Seven

It was no good. No matter how hard Zoe tried to stop herself from yawning the next day, she couldn't. After stumbling back to bed at two o'clock in the morning, still grinning at the memory of the newborn foal's tottering cuteness, she'd fallen into a dreamless sleep. Even so, she'd still spent most of the morning under a fog of tiredness.

Max was confident Fluff's broken leg would heal, so the guinea pig had been fitted with a tiny splint and was living in isolation at the medical center. Worried he would be bored after three days on his own, Zoe had been popping in and out when she could. Fluff didn't seem to notice her exhaustion today, but animal nurse Libby certainly did.

"Are we keeping you awake, Zoe?" she asked with a grin when Zoe yawned for the sixth time in five minutes.

Zoe rubbed at her eyes. "Sorry. Dad took me to see Candy have her new foal and I guess the late night is catching up with me."

"Wow, you got to see a live birth?" Libby asked. "That was lucky!"

"I know," Zoe said, feeling a thrill of excitement in spite of her tiredness. "It was amazing."

"And look at this little guy," Libby said, topping off Fluff's food. "He's doing great."

"It doesn't seem to be bothering him," Zoe replied, peering down at the white microtape holding the guinea pig's leg straight. "When does Max think he'll be able to rejoin the others?"

"In a few more weeks," a male voice answered, causing both Libby and Zoe to turn around.

It was Max and, judging from the tired look on his face, he felt every bit as exhausted as Zoe.

"Once I'm sure the bones have knitted back together cleanly."

"Good," Zoe said, as Fluff let out a mournful little meep. "I bet he misses everyone."

"Probably," Max agreed. "Guinea pigs are very sociable animals. Did you know that in some Scandinavian countries, it's illegal to keep just one on its own?"

Zoe stared at him in astonishment. "Really? You have to have two?"

"At least two," Max said, grinning. "A pet store or breeder can't sell you one on its own unless you can prove you already have another. So there are matchmaking services designed to make sure guinea pigs don't go without a playmate!"

"No way," breathed Zoe, trying to imagine what a guinea-pig dating agency would be like. "How cool!"

"Fluff doesn't need anything like that," Libby said, laughing. "He's got plenty of friends waiting for him back at Guinea Pig Central."

Glancing at the clock, Zoe nodded. "I should get over there, actually. Paolo found a loose wire in the run and he thinks it must have trapped Fluff's leg. He probably broke it trying to get free. But it's all fixed now so we're moving them back in today."

"Excellent news," Max said. "It's a good thing he found the problem so quickly or more of the guinea pigs might have been hurt."

"And it's very lucky you found Fluff so fast," Libby added. "You saved his life."

Max shook his head. "I'm sorry if you thought I blamed you, Zoe. I realized pretty quickly that you're great with animals."

Zoe felt herself blush. "At least it's safe now-ow-ow!" She covered her mouth, embarrassed as it stretched into yet another enormous yawn.

"You can catch up on your sleep tonight," Max said.

Zoe finished her yawn and nodded hard. "As long as Rory's nightmares don't keep us all awake again."

"Yes, your parents mentioned he was having trouble settling in," Max said.

"He thinks there's something in the walls," Zoe admitted. "We all thought he was imagining it but I could have sworn I heard noises last night too."

Max stared at her for a moment, then slapped his palm against his forehead.

"The squirrels, of course! I'm sorry, Zoe, I should have realized earlier."

Now it was Zoe's turn to look confused. "Realized what?"

"There is a family of flying squirrels that live behind the walls of the manor. We haven't wanted to disturb their nest, which is why they're still there, but they can sometimes be noisy," Max said. "I'm not surprised Rory has heard them."

"Squirrels?" Zoe repeated in surprise.

"Northern flying squirrels," Max elaborated. "It's where the stories about Tanglewood being haunted come from. But don't worry, I've never seen a ghost in the manor!"

"Right," Zoe said slowly.

She thought back to how Rory had described his ghost. A rustling in the walls, he'd said, which would fit perfectly with a family of squirrels running around behind the wooden panels! But if Max knew what was making the noise then Oliver must know too – he'd lived in the house, after all. So why hadn't he told Zoe when he'd found out Rory was upset?

Or had he been about to, before Zoe had accidentally reminded him about his mom?

"I really am very sorry," Max said, seeing Zoe's frown. "Come on, why don't we go and explain to Rory? He won't be so worried when he sees how cute they are."

Zoe stifled another yawn. Could the end of their sleepless nights be in sight? She hoped so.

They found Rory and Mrs. Fox in the manor garden. Rory was playing with his cars while Mrs. Fox argued on the phone. There'd been a huge mix-up with the concrete in the otters' pool, meaning that it hadn't set in time for the painters to give it a special waterproof coating, and the weather forecast didn't look good for the next few days. Max and Zoe waited patiently for her to finish.

"Mom, listen, we've got something to tell you," Zoe said as soon as her mother ended the call.

Mrs. Fox rubbed her eyes in an exhausted way.

"Is it important? We're having a nightmare, as you probably heard."

"Speaking of nightmares," Zoe said, taking Rory's hand, "I think you'll both be interested in this."

The two of them listened to Max's explanation about the squirrels. When he stopped talking, Rory looked a long way from convinced.

"Why don't we hear them during the day?" he said.

"Flying squirrels are nocturnal, which means they're only active at night," Max said. He pulled out his phone and tapped at the screen to bring up a picture for Zoe and Rory to look at. "Look at how bushy their tails are."

"Oh, how cute!" Zoe exclaimed, taking in the rodent's black eyes, long whiskers and round ears.

"Do they really fly?" Rory asked.

"This says that flying squirrels glide," Zoe said, reading the words beneath the photo. "A special membrane between their front and back legs spreads out to help them glide through the air between trees. They use their legs to steer, and their tails as brakes when they want to stop."

Max nodded. "These squirrels can glide between trees for more than 150 feet at a time!"

Zoe glanced at Rory. He was touching the screen, swiping between pictures of the flying squirrels, completely absorbed by the cute creatures. She didn't think they'd have any trouble getting him to bed tonight.

Mom sighed. "Something else that needs to be taken care of. And squirrels can be very destructive — I'm not sure I'm happy with them living in the house. What if they chew through an electrical cable? Wouldn't they be better off in their natural habitat?"

"We have tried removing them but they always come back," Max said. "But we could put down traps again if you'd like?"

Traps? Zoe's head jerked up in horror. Max saw her expression and hurried to reassure her. "Safe traps," he said. "Boxes where they get caught inside so that we can release them into the woods."

Relieved, Zoe nodded. "Oh, okay. I suppose those kind of traps are fine." She gazed at the wall wistfully. "Although now that I know they're there, I like the idea of getting to know our cute neighbors."

Mrs. Fox shook her head. "Don't get any ideas," she warned. "The chances are they'll be moving out."

Zoe thought about arguing but she knew the expression on her mother's face well: her mind was made up. Suddenly Rory looked up from Max's phone.

"I like flying squirrels," he said, his eyes bright with excitement. "Is it bedtime yet?"

It started to rain in the afternoon, fat heavy raindrops that the weather forecast said were set to stay for a couple of days. Zoe wasn't about to let a bit of rain stop her from seeing Candy and Flash, though – it would take a hurricane to keep her away from her favorite zebras. Right after lunch, she dug out her boots and raincoat and splashed her way over to the barn.

Posters starring Flash had begun to appear around the park: *Meet Tanglewood's Latest Zooborn!* Zoe knew her parents planned to set up a webcam so that animal lovers could see him and Candy online, and photographs had already appeared on the park's website. Some people had left enthusiastic comments under the pictures – it seemed as though Flash was a big hit even before the grand reopening in just over a week's time.

The barn was quiet. Candy turned her head from the hay basket as Zoe entered, her black eyes watchful. Flash was standing up with no trace of wobbliness now. He butted determinedly at his mother's tummy, looking for milk. His fuzzy fur wasn't as sleek as Candy's and he had brown-tinged stripes instead of pure black, although Zoe knew they'd change color as he grew. It was hard to believe that he was less than a day old.

Flash's slightly-too-big ears pricked forwards as she came closer – she knew zebras had excellent hearing but Flash seemed very alert for such a young foal. Then again, in the wild, he'd need to be – who knew when a predator might attack?

"Hello, you two," she said in a gentle voice, leaning over the enclosure fence with a warm smile. "How are you both?"

Flash continued to guzzle milk, showing no signs of fear. Zoe grinned.

"Typical baby," she said to Candy, thinking back to how Rory had been when he was tiny. "Only interested in one thing."

She stood in silence for a few minutes, enjoying the way Candy fussed over her foal and the look on Flash's face as he put up with it. The grooming helped the pair of them to bond, so that Flash would recognize his mother's stripes when they rejoined the other zebras, and Zoe loved watching them get to know each other. No wonder people were excited about visiting Candy and Flash – they were the cutest sight ever!

"We should have called you Twinkle," Zoe said, smiling as Flash lay down and rolled around in the straw. "Because you're definitely going to be the star attraction when we reopen!"

She tried hard not to mind when Oliver walked into the barn. He had just as much right to be there as she did – helping with the zebras was one of his duties, after all.

"Wow, Flash is doing so well," he said as he got closer.

He sounded delighted and proud, and so different from the sulky Oliver she was used to, that Zoe blinked. Letting him name the foal had obviously worked exactly as she'd hoped. And she agreed – Flash *was* doing well.

"He's wonderful," she said, gazing at the zebras. "Candy looks very proud too."

It was true – the zebra had a contented air about her, almost as though she knew she'd done a good job.

"Jenna says they'll need a few more days in isolation and then she'll take Flash to meet the herd," Oliver told her. "I'm really looking forward to it."

"Me too," Zoe said, picturing Flash frolicking with the other zebras. She glanced sideways at Oliver. "Your dad told us about the flying squirrel nest in the walls."

"I know you won't believe me but I am sorry I scared Rory," he said, and Zoe thought he looked it.

"I should have explained what the noise was."

"Yes, you should." Realizing how upset she sounded, Zoe softened her voice. "Rory is beyond excited. I think he wants to adopt them."

Oliver grinned. "Huh, I bet your mom would love that."

"Between the guinea pigs, the rabbits and all the other small animals, she thinks we have enough to look after," Zoe said.

"Yeah, it's better to look after a few animals properly than a lot of them badly."

His lip curled as he said the last word and he looked away. Zoe stared at him in confusion. Was that another dig at her, because Fluff had been hurt? Was he suggesting she'd looked after him badly?

"I know you think I'm useless with animals but your dad doesn't. He told me earlier that he thinks I'm great with them."

Now it was Oliver's turn to stare. "What?"

His expression was innocent but his eyes were guilty. Zoe felt her temper start to slip. "You know what I mean. I heard what you said to your dad. You made it sound like Fluff's injury might have been my fault."

Oliver's eyes narrowed. "I don't know what you're talking about."

"I heard you!" Zoe burst out, causing Candy and Flash's ears to flatten against their heads.

"Keep your voice down, you'll upset the zebras," Oliver hissed. "And of course Dad said you were good – you're the boss's daughter! He has to be nice to you."

Zoe gasped.

"You're jealous. You think you know it all and you can't bear the thought of anyone taking over your precious park, even when they're trying to help." She took a deep breath. "You don't own Tanglewood."

Two spots of deep rosy red appeared on his cheeks. "Wow. You really are a spoiled brat, Zoe," he snapped over his shoulder as he walked out of the barn. "Talk to me again when you've grown up a bit."

Zoe watched him leave, her anger draining away

to leave a strange sick feeling in the pit of her stomach. He was right, she realized. She *did* sound spoiled. But there was just something about Oliver that brought out the worst in her.

Chapter Eight

It rained hard overnight. Zoe woke up several times listening to the raindrops lashing against her window. Even the squirrels seemed subdued – she couldn't hear them scratching around the walls like they usually did. She snuggled underneath her covers in the dark, hoping Flash wasn't scared by the rain rattling on the barn roof. Then again, he had Candy to cuddle up to if he felt afraid.

The bad weather continued for hours, making

Zoe glad it was her day off. She played games with Rory and watched some TV but she soon grew bored. By the time the rain stopped she was desperate to get out of the house.

"Why don't you go and see the penguins?" Mom suggested, as Zoe sighed for the hundredth time. "If you're lucky, you might just catch feeding time."

"Feel like a snack?" Nick, the penguin keeper, called from behind the glass-walled enclosure when Zoe arrived. He held up a bucket.

Zoe grinned as hordes of penguins waddled towards him, their beady eyes fixed on their lunch. They were so cute and comical.

"No, thanks. It looks like you've got plenty of mouths to feed already."

Nick thrust a gloved hand into the bucket and scattered silvery fish into the water. "I could do with some help, actually. If you're not too busy?"

Zoe watched the birds dive in to scoop up the

food. She'd seen penguins plenty of times at her old zoo but she'd never had the chance to feed them before.

"Yes please," she said, pushing up the sleeves of her raincoat. "What would you like me to do?"

Waiting until she'd pulled on a plastic apron and some rubber gloves, Nick handed Zoe a much smaller bucket of fish.

"Dinner is served," he said, with a funny little flourish. "Did you know that Humboldt penguins swallow their fish whole, without even chewing?"

Zoe hadn't known. She dug her scoop into the fish and threw them into the shimmering blue pond, watching in fascination as a nearby penguin swooped in front of her and gulped one down, head first. They were so graceful in the water, completely different from on land.

"What kind of fish do they like?"

"In the wild, they'll eat krill and other sea creatures. We feed them these anchovies and they're the perfect size for swallowing whole."

Zoe nodded. "Is it true that their feet never freeze?"

Nick grinned. "Not these penguins – they come from the coast of Chile in South America."

"Oh," Zoe said, blinking in confusion. "I thought they all came from cold places like Antarctica."

"Some breeds do – the emperor and the king penguins, for example," Nick said. "But where I come from in South Africa, we see them on the beaches all the time. Only the ones from really cold places can control the blood flow to their feet, so that they're almost the same temperature as the ice. So yes, it's true – *their* feet don't freeze."

She listened as Nick explained more about the different types of penguins and what they were doing at Tanglewood to breed the Humboldts – they were a threatened species in their natural habitat so it was important to make sure there was a healthy population in captivity.

"You'll be able to see some chicks hatching soon," Nick said as he poured the last of the fish into the water. "The next breeding season starts in September."

The thought of September made Zoe's stomach somersault. She'd be starting her new school then, without a single friend. With an enemy, in fact, if she and Oliver couldn't stop squabbling.

"When there are a few chicks, they open a nursery," Nick went on. "In the wild, the chicks' fur isn't waterproof immediately so the parents take turns looking after them. Penguins are very sociable birds."

Unlike me and Oliver, Zoe thought with embarrassment. The trouble was every time she tried to be friendly, he threw it back in her face. Then again, she hadn't been very friendly yesterday – she'd called him a know-it-all and accused him of acting like he owned the park. No wonder he'd stormed off.

Sighing, she handed the empty bucket back to Nick.

"I don't suppose you've seen Oliver today, have you?" she asked, stripping off her rubber gloves.

"He was here earlier," Nick said. "You must have just missed him. I think he said he was heading home – you might find him at the cottage if you need to speak to him. Do you know how to get there?"

Zoe listened carefully to Nick's directions and thanked him for letting her help. Then she set off for Max's cottage. Oliver had said some pretty nasty things but she hadn't behaved fantastically either. Maybe it was time they *both* grew up a bit.

The sun had come out, chasing the grumbling gray rain clouds away, and the windows of Magpie Cottage were open. As Zoe reached the front door, she heard raised voices.

"We've been over this, Oliver." Max sounded weary. "Tanglewood was in danger of closing down for good until Mr. and Mrs. Fox came along. They're not our enemies, they are the breath of fresh air this place needs."

"But they're changing everything!" Oliver replied, the words ringing with furious resentment.

"Of course they're changing things," Max said.

"The park was old and needed updating, half the enclosures were falling down. Even you must understand that we have to put the animals' needs first – nothing stays the same forever."

"Why?" Oliver exploded. "Why can't things stay the same?"

Max sighed. "Oliver—"

"No! I'm tired of you saying I'll get used to stuff. I hate the Foxes and I wish they'd never come!"

A door slammed and Zoe heard the thud of feet. Horrified, she realized the sound was coming towards her. She began to back away just as the front door was wrenched open and Oliver stormed out, almost knocking her over. For a moment, he looked shocked to see her and Zoe was taken aback to see tears in his eyes. Then he blinked hard and his face twisted into a bitter scowl.

"I hope you heard all that."

He brushed past her and vanished around the corner. Shaken, Zoe stared after him.

"I'm so sorry, Zoe," Max said, appearing in the

doorway. "For what it's worth, I don't think Oliver really hates you and your family. He's struggling with a lot of things – we both are."

He gave a sad smile and Zoe realized that Max must miss his wife just as much as Oliver missed his mom. "It's okay," she said. "I understand."

"Thank you," the vet said, and sighed. "Now, what can I do for you?"

Zoe hesitated. If she told Max everything then maybe Oliver would stop taunting her and she would stop losing her temper. But that would mean getting him into even worse trouble and he'd only dislike her more.

She gazed at Max, noticing the dark circles under his eyes and the way his mouth turned down at the corners.

"It doesn't matter," she said, turning away so he didn't see her own unhappiness. "See you later, Max."

Chapter Nine

The temperature soared over the next week. Zoe felt as if she was sizzling as she hurried from enclosure to enclosure, carrying plants, helping to arrange rock displays and settling the smaller animals into their new homes, ready for Tanglewood to open its gates.

The weather wasn't the only thing that was overheating – tempers were at boiling point as the countdown to reopening got shorter. Dolly had banned the few remaining builders from the cafe because their boots made her new floor dirty, a vital shipment of plants for the gibbon gym had gone missing and the delays over Tindu the tiger's paperwork meant that no one could even guess when he might be joining Tanglewood. By the time the morning before the grand reopening arrived, Mr. and Mrs. Fox were tearing their hair out and Zoe was doing her best to keep out of everyone's way.

"Come on," she whispered to Rory as both their parents were arguing with different people on their cellphones. "Let's get out of here."

They bumped into Max at the gate between the house and the park. He looked every bit as stressed as all the other adults but at least he stopped to smile at them.

"Hello, you two. How are things?"

"Shouty," Rory said immediately. "I can't hear the squirrels."

Max laughed. "Everything is a little crazy at the moment, it's not much fun." He glanced at Zoe and his expression softened. "I'm just off on my rounds – want to join me?"

Zoe nodded. "Yes, please. Who are you going to see first?"

"There's a lorikeet with a damaged wing over in the aviary," Max said. "Do you know what a lorikeet is, Rory?"

"A type of parrot," Rory replied, faster than a snake. "It comes from Australia."

Max grinned. "Exactly right."

Rory looked like he might pop with excitement and Zoe felt a flutter of anticipation too.

"Are you going to see Candy?" she asked.

She'd stayed away from the zebra and her foal in case Oliver was there – after hearing the argument between him and Max, Zoe had decided to keep her distance.

Max smiled. "I'm sure we can squeeze in a visit later."

As they reached the aviary Max explained that the lorikeet had flown into a branch and hurt its wing. "It's been bandaged and splinted for the last eight weeks," he said, letting them into a small building at the rear of the enclosure.

"Like Fluff's leg," Zoe said.

"Exactly," Max said. "Except that for Buster it's meant that he hasn't been able to fly. Today, we're going to take the splint off and let him stretch his wings, see if he remembers what to do."

The lorikeet was in a small cage on a table in one corner of the brightly lit room. He eyed them beadily and hopped sideways along his pole to get a closer look. Zoe was amazed at the jewel-like colors of his feathers – his head was bright blue but his chest and neck were orange and yellow. His wings were green, although one was covered by a frayed white bandage, and his beak was ruby red.

"He really is a rainbow," she said in admiration.

"He's had a good try at pulling his bandage off," Max noted. "Let's scrub up and we can take a closer look."

The three of them washed and dried their hands.

Max opened his medical bag and pulled out some slender silver scissors. "Do you know what lorikeets eat?"

Rory squinted up his face in thought. "Seeds?"

"Not seeds," Max said. "Lorikeets have a sweet tooth, so they like nectar and pollen from flowers. Once I've made sure Buster's wing has completely healed, I want to see if he can fly well before I let him out into the aviary with the other birds. I'll need your help with that."

Rory looked like all his dreams had come true. "Really?"

"Really," Max said, his eyes twinkling. "But for now, why don't you perch on that table and stay as quiet as you can?"

Zoe led her brother to the white table and they watched intently as Max opened the cage and cupped his hand around Buster. The lorikeet let out an indignant squawk but stayed calm. The scissors flashed as Max snipped away the bandage and removed the splint from the damaged wing. He stretched the green feathers out, moving his fingers carefully along the wing, before folding it back in and looking up.

"Everything feels fine," he announced, looking satisfied. "Zoe, if you open the refrigerator next to you, you should see some little white tubs. Could you take two out, please?"

Zoe jumped up and did as she was told. The refrigerator was stocked with all kinds of tubs but she saw the ones Max meant right away – two tiny round tubs covered with plastic lids, labeled with that day's date.

"These?" she asked, holding them up.

"That's right," Max said. "They're fresh nectar containers. We're going to give Buster here a treat."

Following the vet's instructions, Zoe removed the lids. The containers were filled with a speckled green liquid.

"Now, each of you take one and go and stand at the end of the room. Hold it out and if you stay very calm and still, Buster will fly towards you and land on your arm."

Zoe led Rory to the end of the room.

"Don't put your fingers in it," she warned, guessing he was tempted to try the sweet treat for himself. "You're not a lorikeet!"

"*Squawk!*" said Rory, poking out his tongue.

"Ready?" Max called.

Zoe and Rory held out their containers.

"Ready!" they chorused.

Max lowered the hand covering Buster's wings. For a moment, the bird didn't move. Then he gave a little shake and tipped his head to the side, as though realizing something had changed. His beak nipped at the feathers of his healed wing, rearranging them as he whistled. With a little hop, he flapped carefully, testing the wing. And then he launched himself into the air, flapping hard to gain height, and Zoe saw that the inside of his wings were just as pretty as the outside, yellow and blue and orange.

"Hold your nectar up," she whispered to Rory. "And don't move."

A second later, Buster seemed to notice the food.

He swooped down and landed daintily on Rory's outstretched arm, dipping his beak into the sticky green liquid.

"Wow!" Rory said, staring at the bird in delight. "Hello, Buster."

Max told Zoe to move to another part of the room so that Buster would fly to her and sure enough, he did. She held her breath as the lorikeet balanced on her hand – his claws tickled as they gripped her skin and his feathers were even prettier close up. He pecked at the nectar, guzzling it down as though he hadn't eaten for days.

"He's hungry," she said with a grin.

"He's greedy," Max snorted. "But he's had a tough few weeks so we'll let him off."

After a few more swoops, Max seemed satisfied that Buster's wing was mended. Zoe had wondered how Max was going to catch the bird but she needn't have worried – the vet simply cupped the bird in one hand while he was snacking and held him carefully to prevent him from flapping.

"Buster's used to being handled," he said. "Another side effect of a hurt wing, I'm afraid."

In the aviary, Buster fluttered into the midst of the other birds, chirping and squawking.

"He's telling them all about his adventures," Zoe said, laughing.

"Probably," Max said. "I think he's going to be fine. Should we leave him to it?"

They waved goodbye to the lorikeets. Zoe hoped they'd be visiting Flash next – she couldn't wait to see how much he'd grown. But before she could ask Max where they were heading, his radio crackled. He listened carefully, a frown creasing his forehead. Then he sighed.

"There's a problem with Sinbad's paw," he said. "I need to head straight over to Big Cat Mountain."

"I hope he's okay," Zoe said. "Is it serious?"

Max shook his head. "I don't think so but I'll know more when I see him. Why don't you two head over to see Candy and we can meet up again later? I think Flash is old enough to meet Rory now."

"Okay," Zoe said, hoping she wouldn't run into Oliver. Then again, she couldn't avoid him forever.

"Come on, Rory, let's go and see the zebras. I think you're going to love Flash!"

"Flash is just the cutest," Zoe told Rory as they arrived at the stable block where Candy and her foal were staying. "He hasn't grown into his ears yet and his stripes are still a tiny bit brow—"

She stopped dead, staring around the enclosure in confusion. It was empty, swept clean of straw. There was no sign of Candy or her foal.

"Excuse me, Jenna," Zoe said, trying not to sound panicky as she hurried up to the keeper. "Where are Candy and Flash?"

"Hi, Zoe, hi, Rory," Jenna replied, smiling. "We decided it was time to introduce Flash to the herd today so a couple of the other keepers have taken him and Candy back to the zebra field."

"Oh!" Zoe burst out in disappointment. "I wish I could have helped."

Jenna's smile faded. "I'm sorry, Zoe. Oliver said he'd already asked you and you'd said no."

Oliver! Zoe felt her insides explode with frustration and anger. She shook her head, trying to keep a lid on her temper.

"He didn't ask me. I would have jumped at the chance – I love Candy and Flash."

"I'm really sorry," Jenna repeated and she looked it. "Oliver must have gotten his wires crossed somehow. But maybe if you go now, you can still help."

Oliver hadn't gotten his wires crossed at all, Zoe thought furiously. Determined not to let him get away with this, Zoe took a deep calming breath and forced herself to smile.

"Great idea. Come on, Rory, I'd better take you back to Mom."

Rory grumbled all the way back to the house but Zoe bribed him with a promise to go and visit Sinbad later. Then she ran to the zebra field. Even if there wasn't anything obvious to do she'd find something, she vowed, just to see the look on Oliver's face. He'd told her to grow up but it was time he learned how to share Tanglewood with her.

Oliver was standing by the fence of the field, watching the other zebras fuss around Candy and Flash. A couple of other keepers were standing on the far side of the enclosure, out of earshot. Zoe didn't waste any time: she marched straight up to Oliver, arms folded.

"Why did you tell Jenna I didn't want to help with Candy's move?"

"I saw you and my dad with the lorikeets," he said, not looking at her. "It looked like you were having too much fun to help us."

She stared at him. It almost sounded like he was jealous of her spending time with his father.

"What is your problem? Why do you hate us so much?"

"I don't hate *all* of you," Oliver said. "Just the one who thinks she's better than everyone else."

"What's that supposed to mean?" Zoe demanded. "You've hardly spoken to me since I arrived – how do you know what I think about *anything*?"

"I don't need to speak to you," he snapped. "Even an idiot could see you think you're Little Miss Perfect."

Zoe shook her head. "I don't. Really—"

"Shut up!" Oliver yelled, right into her face. "It's not just me, anyway. No one likes you."

"That's not true," Zoe shouted back, clenching her fists.

"It is. People are only polite to you because they have to be." A wicked gleam entered his eyes. "Haven't you noticed that you hardly ever work with the same keepers? They take turns at having to put up with you. You're the park joke."

There was a roaring in Zoe's ears. It was true that she worked with lots of different people around the park but she'd assumed that was simply to do with work patterns and who needed help the most. She'd never stopped to think that the keepers might not want her around, that she was more of a hindrance than a help.

"That's not true," she said, swallowing hard. "I know plenty about animal care."

He raised his eyebrows in disbelief. "Oh yeah? Tell that to Fluff!"

Zoe gasped. When was he going to let that go?

"Everyone knows Fluff's broken leg was caused by a loose wire. What other lies have you told about me?"

Oliver opened his mouth to reply but Zoe stormed on. "I've had enough of your bullying. I know you stole my bag and threw it on the dung heap. And you terrified Rory!"

He glared at her. "I told you that was an accident."

"I don't believe you," Zoe said. "You're horrible, Oliver Chambers, and I've had enough of it. I'm telling my parents everything."

"Oh boohoo," he sneered. "Go crying to your mommy and daddy then, see if I care."

The words rang with defiance but there was a definite hint of nervousness behind them.

"Just stay away from me," Zoe said, pointing a shaking finger at him. "From all of us, actually."

"Don't worry," Oliver snarled over his shoulder as he walked away. "I will!"

Zoe's eyes stung with unshed tears as she stared at Candy and Flash, nuzzling among the other zebras. When her parents had told her they'd bought Tanglewood, she'd felt like the luckiest person in the world – her wildest dreams had come true.

But Oliver seemed determined to spoil things for her. And she had no idea how to stop him.

Chapter Ten

The scene in the kitchen had hardly changed when Zoe walked back in just before lunch. The breakfast dishes were still on the table, her mom hadn't brushed her hair and both her parents were talking into their cellphones. Rory was sitting on the floor, doing an animal puzzle.

"The park reopens tomorrow," Zoe heard her father say in a harassed voice, "and we still don't have a working train for the miniature railroad.

When do you think you can get the new engine part over to us?"

"I don't care how much it costs," Mrs. Fox said into her phone. "I've got a major aphid problem and I need two hundred ladybugs sent over this afternoon. Can you help?"

Zoe listened for a few seconds, waiting for one of them to finish their conversation so that she could tell them about Oliver, but they were both so engrossed they had hardly noticed she was there. Sighing, she took Rory's hand.

"Why don't we go upstairs and listen for the squirrels?"

They were almost at the stairs when Mom called them back.

"Zoe? Is everything okay?"

Zoe paused, gnawing her lip. Should she pretend that everything was fine or tell her parents what had been going on with Oliver? It might make her feel better to get things out in the open…

"Zoe?" Mom asked again, studying her.

This was her chance, Zoe thought, the perfect opportunity to tell her mother everything.

"What?" Dad's voice floated through from the kitchen. "How am I supposed to run the Tanglewood Express with no engine?"

And Zoe realized she couldn't do it – not when her parents were so stressed about tomorrow's grand reopening. They had plenty to worry about already and adding her problems with Oliver to the load didn't seem fair. Besides, she was determined not to let him spoil things more than he already had.

"Everything's fine," she said, trying her best to sound normal.

"Good," Mrs. Fox said with a smile. "Now, can you play with your brother for a while? I've got a few more calls I really have to make."

"Yeah," Zoe said, glad to be able to help. "Come on, Rory. We've got some squirrels to track down."

The next morning, Zoe woke up before her alarm. She lay there for a moment, wondering why her stomach was fluttering with excitement and then she remembered – it was opening day! Pushing back the covers, she found her slippers under the bed and hurried downstairs.

It had rained again overnight, and the grass glistened emerald green through the kitchen window. Mom was sitting at the table, cradling a cup of coffee as she pored over some paperwork.

"Morning," Zoe said, kissing her on the cheek. "Have you been sitting here all night?"

"Not quite," Mom said, making a face. "Although it feels like I have. There's so much to think about. I think today will be the craziest day yet."

Zoe nodded. "What time will Auntie Nina be here?"

"About ten o'clock, I think," Mrs. Fox said, checking the clock on the wall.

The plan was that Rory would spend the day with Auntie Nina and their cousins, leaving Zoe free to help out where needed. *And to avoid Oliver*, Zoe thought, but she was trying not to waste time worrying about him.

"Mom," she said quietly, feeling the now-familiar knot of dread in her stomach whenever she thought about Oliver. "We did the right thing coming here, didn't we?"

Her mother lowered her cup and stared at her. "Of course we did. What made you ask that?"

Zoe looked away. "I don't know. It's just you and Dad are working so hard and you look worried all the time. Actually, I don't know about Dad so much because I've hardly seen him, but you spend a lot of time on the phone and –" she hesitated, unsure whether to say what was on her mind – "it made me wonder whether we'd all be happier if we'd never come here, that's all."

Mom stood and pulled Zoe into a hug. "I'm sorry, sweetheart, things have been so hectic that we haven't had much time for you and Rory lately." She sighed. "It won't always be like this, I promise.

Everything will be easier once we're open. We'll be able to relax a little then."

Zoe hugged her mother back, certain she'd made the right decision to keep Oliver's behavior to herself, at least until tomorrow.

"Good," she said, smiling. "And you don't need to worry about today – it's going to be totally roarsome!"

Mom laughed. "What a perfect way to describe Tanglewood. We might have to put that on our posters!"

Out in the park, there were people everywhere. The keepers wore sharp green polo shirts with the brand-new Team Tanglewood logo her parents had designed. Other workers wore crisp white shirts – Zoe guessed they would be working at the park gates, selling tickets and handing out maps to the visitors.

The main gates now had a new coat of glossy black paint and the roaring lions that overlooked them had been cleaned and repaired. Bold signposts had appeared everywhere, directing visitors into Tanglewood and how to get around once there. The only signs of the building work were a few diggers, tucked away behind painted wooden fences until the park had closed again later and they could be taken away. Zoe felt a glow of pride as she gazed around: Tanglewood was looking great!

As Zoe passed the cafe, she waved and Dolly bustled over to the door.

"Your dad was looking for you, did you see him? He's over at the medical center."

"Thanks," Zoe called.

She had a long list of jobs to do, including one final check that Guinea Pig Central was clean and neat, but that could wait. It was only just eight o'clock; the park wouldn't be open for ninety minutes yet.

Dad was chatting with Max when Zoe slipped into the medical center.

"Dolly said you were looking for me," she called. "Is everything okay?"

"Fine," Mr. Fox said. He held a plastic-wrapped package. "I just wanted to give you this."

Frowning, Zoe took it. "What is it?"

Dad grinned. "Your uniform. Max has been telling me how helpful you've been over the last few weeks and I know how hard you've worked. So we decided you should have your very own Team Tanglewood shirt, like all the other keepers."

Zoe let out an excited squeal.

"Really?" she said, her heart bursting with pride. "My own shirt?"

"Try it on," Max suggested, his eyes twinkling. "It's the smallest one we could find, so I hope it fits."

Zoe didn't need to be told twice. She hurried into a bathroom stall and swapped the old T-shirt she'd tugged on earlier for the polo shirt. It fit perfectly. She stood for a moment taking in her reflection in the mirror. Her parents had brought animal merchandise home from the zoo in the past but she'd never been treated like a member of staff before! It was a proud moment – surely Oliver couldn't claim she was the park joke now?

"Perfect," Max said, when she came back out to show them. "Now you really look like part of the team."

"Thank you," Zoe said, smoothing the green material against her shorts. "I love it."

Dad squeezed her hand. "I'm proud of you. Great work."

Zoe beamed at him in delight. This was shaping up to be the best day ever!

Max checked his watch. "I'd better get over to Big Cat Mountain."

"And I've got an appointment with Team GP," Zoe said, remembering where she had been going. She flashed a smile at Max and her dad. "Catch you later!"

After she'd made sure the guinea-pig enclosure was fully stocked and spotless, Zoe headed over to the zebra field to stock up the animal feed stall there. Zoe was grateful for the peace – she wanted a few calm minutes with Flash before the crowds arrived and made it impossible. She hoped the little foal wouldn't be worried by the noise and hubbub of the park visitors – he was still very young after all. But she already knew he was going to be a huge hit. Who could resist a gorgeous baby zebra?

The zebras were at the far end of the enclosure – she counted eight in all. Some were huddled protectively around Candy and Flash, others were sniffing around the shiny new water troughs the plumbers had installed. As Zoe leaned on the fence to get a better look, she saw something glinting in the half-dried mud. She stared hard. It looked like a small spike of metal sticking up out of the ground. Whatever it was, she knew it wasn't supposed to be there. All it would take was one carelessly placed hoof and one of the zebras could be badly hurt. And with so many people coming to Tanglewood just to see Flash, it would be a disaster if the zebras weren't on display.

Park protocol demanded that the keepers and assistants never entered any large animal pen alone, no matter how experienced they were, and Zoe knew she should go for help. But everyone was so busy and the shiny object was so close – surely she could slip through the gate and investigate first?

Making up her mind, she undid the lock and was through the gate in seconds. The zebras watched her curiously. By the time she'd reached the piece of metal, she knew she'd done the right thing. It was a long thin screw, with a vicious-looking point. Reaching down, she tugged it out of the mud and zipped it into her pocket. *The plumbers must have dropped it*, she decided, glancing around and checking for any more.

When she was satisfied there was nothing else that might endanger the zebras, she began to walk back to the gate. Flash lifted his head to watch and came trotting towards her, his ears pricked forwards. Zoe laughed as his black nose nuzzled her pockets, searching for a treat.

"Sorry, boy, I don't have anything for you at the

moment," she said, ruffling his mane. "But I do need to check the supplies on the animal feed stand so maybe I'll bring you something back. Would you like that?"

As if on cue, the little foal snorted softly. Zoe laughed. "I'll take that as a yes. Wait here."

She started to make her way back to the gate. The foal followed.

"Stay there," Zoe said, grinning. "Goodness, you're bold."

Flash didn't take his eyes off her as she slipped through the gate, pulled it closed and crossed to the wooden push-along stand not far from the field. Bending down, she opened the doors underneath the counter and peered inside. There was a cluster of neatly tied paper bags full of tasty fresh animal feed, not intended for the zebras – there were signs all over the park saying which animals could be fed and which could not – but visitors could buy a bag to give to the other animals, where the signs allowed. Zoe counted the bags – not nearly enough for the busy day ahead. She'd better get some more.

She straightened up. Flash seemed to have lost interest in her and was butting his nose gently along the gate.

"Back soon," she called and set off.

At the food store, Zoe loaded a basket with fresh feed bags. She stuffed a carrot into her pocket for Flash and headed back to the zebra field. A familiar figure was next to the fence as she approached it and Zoe felt her heart sink: Oliver. He was wearing a Tanglewood polo shirt too, just like hers. She slowed down, wondering if she could do another job on her list to avoid him but just as she was about to decide, she saw him lift his radio.

"This is Oliver, is anyone there?" he said. "Please respond, over."

Zoe frowned. Was it her imagination or did he sound a bit panic-stricken?

Oliver spoke again. "Has anyone been in with the zebras today? The gate is open and I can't find Flash."

Zoe froze, her heart thudding hard and fast.

Had she heard correctly? Had Oliver said he couldn't find Flash?

"I repeat," Oliver said, and this time there was no mistaking the panic in his voice, "Flash the foal is missing from the field. I can't see him anywhere!"

Chapter Eleven

Zoe ran. Her eyes scanned the grassy enclosure, seeking out the foal and hoping Oliver was wrong. By the time she reached the fence, she knew with a terrible breathless certainty that he wasn't. Candy was swinging her head left and right, searching for her baby. But how could Flash be missing? Ten minutes ago he'd been right there.

"What happened?" she said. "How could he have escaped?"

For a moment, she thought Oliver wouldn't answer. Then he grunted. "The gate was open. Someone must have left the safety lock off."

An icy squeeze of dread gripped Zoe's heart. Had she left the gate open?

"The safety lock?"

"The extra one that goes on the gate," Oliver said, looking at her as though she'd grown another head. "We always double lock the animal enclosures, you know that."

A strange buzzing started in Zoe's ears as she thought back to when she'd left the field. Had she simply slid the bolt home or had there been a safety lock to hook through the bolt afterwards? She would have noticed if the safety lock had been missing... wouldn't she?

"Who knows how long he's been gone?" Oliver went on. "He could be anywhere in the park."

As one, they turned and hunted around them. There was no sign of the foal. The radio burst into life and Zoe heard her father's voice.

"*Stay there, we're on our way, over.*"

"The last person in must have left the gate open," Oliver said, shaking his head. "It's the only explanation."

Zoe started to tremble. She *had* shut the gate, she knew she had. But she couldn't swear she'd double locked it. And now Flash was missing – lost, maybe even hurt – because of her.

"He was here a few minutes ago…" she murmured.

Oliver stared at her, his eyes narrowing.

"It was you, wasn't it?" he accused. "You went in there and you left the gate open. On your own too – this is your fault!"

"It isn't. I did go in there but I'm sure the gate was closed when I left." Trembling even more, Zoe met his disgusted stare head-on and another thought occurred to her. "How do I know you didn't let Flash out, to make me look bad?"

"That's just ridiculous," Oliver snapped back, just as Jenna, Zoe's dad and Max hurried towards them. "We're not all as sneaky as you, Zoe."

"What happened?" Mr. Fox demanded, his gaze fixed on the field. "Any idea how Flash got out?"

Zoe felt her eyes start to burn. Deep down she knew it was unfair to accuse Oliver of letting the foal out. "I went in to get this," she said, pulling out the metal screw. "It was sticking out of the mud. But I – I can't remember whether I put the safety lock on afterwards."

The three adults stared at her. "I'm glad you found this," her father said, taking the screw. "But you forgot the first Zoo Law I taught you – always double lock the animal gates."

"I know," Zoe said, hanging her head. "It was definitely closed when I left, I know that."

"You shouldn't have been in there alone, anyway," Mr. Fox went on. "Zebras can be dangerous, especially when they have a young one to protect. You could have been hurt."

Zoe stared at the metal screw. What was the point of going in to get it if she'd then left the gate open so that Flash could escape?

"We should lock the gate now, to make sure Candy doesn't go looking for Flash," Max said. He peered at the gate and frowned. "I can't see the extra lock. Where did you leave it, Zoe?"

Others were arriving now, Paolo and Mizbah and Nick and a lot of other keepers Zoe recognized. Even Dolly was there, her usually cheerful face worried. Zoe felt even worse.

"I don't know," she told Max. "I don't even remember seeing it."

Her father shook his head. "It doesn't matter now. What matters is that Flash is out in the park somewhere and needs to be found, before he gets hurt." He checked his watch. "It's less than an hour until the gates open, we need to split into pairs and search everywhere."

"There aren't enough radios to go around," Max said. "Oliver, we'll need yours so the keepers can stay in touch."

Looking even more disgusted, Oliver handed over his radio. Another stab of anxiety hit Zoe as she watched the keepers pair up and decide who was searching where. Less than an hour? That was no time at all and the park couldn't open with a large animal on the loose, especially not its star attraction. Zoe felt her eyes brim with tears – if Tanglewood couldn't open then the day, maybe even the park's future, would be ruined. They'd have to leave and her parents would need to find new jobs. She shook her head and blinked hard. It was all her fault. *Everything* was her fault.

Oliver flashed an impatient look her way.

"There's no use standing there feeling sorry for yourself. Go home if you can't do anything useful."

"Oliver!" Max snapped, glancing up from the rope he was wrapping around the enclosure gate. "That's enough. Stay here with Zoe and keep your eyes open."

"What?" Oliver cried, his eyes widening. "Why can't I go and look for Flash? Nick will take me, won't you?"

Nick shook his head as he and Mizbah hurried off. "Not this time, Oliver. We'll be quicker on our own."

"Paolo?" Oliver called, sounding desperate. "Need another pair of hands?"

"Sorry, Oliver," Paolo said over his shoulder. "But there needs to be two of you here in case Flash comes back. That way one of you can come and find us while the other stays with Flash."

Oliver's lip curled in frustration. "But—"

"No arguments, Oliver," Max said in a steely voice. "We don't have the time."

Deep in discussion, Max and Mr. Fox headed down one of the paths, leaving Oliver and Zoe alone. Feeling sick with worry, Zoe watched them disappear around a bend. What if they couldn't find Flash? What if he was trapped somewhere or hurt? She'd never forgive herself and from the looks of things, neither would her father or anyone else. Heavy-hearted, she picked up the basket of animal food and trudged from the gate to the stand.

Moodily, Oliver followed and watched her, arms folded.

"Go on, say it," Zoe said as she piled the paper bags onto the shelves. "You wish we'd never come here."

"No need to say it," Oliver said. "Anyone can see what a disaster it's been."

"A disaster?" Zoe echoed in disbelief, staring up at him. She got to her feet. "Look around. You see all the new enclosures, each one carefully designed to be eco-friendly and perfect for the animals inside? The just-painted signs and stronger fences? The freshly laid paths so that visitors get a better view of the animals? That all happened because my parents took over Tanglewood and paid for all the work. They care about this place and everything in it." She took a deep breath. "No one else seems to think it's a disaster. Only you."

"Wait until the gates don't open on time," Oliver argued. "Wait until all the roads are clogged up with cars trying to get in and there are angry people demanding their money back. Wait until the grand reopening is a total flop!"

Zoe took a deep shuddering breath. She wouldn't cry in front of him, not if she could help it.

"Then we might have to leave and you'll get what you want. But if we go, you and everyone who works here and all the animals will have to leave too. Have you thought about that?"

She could tell from his sudden silence that he hadn't. He scowled at her, as though trying to think of more insults, then turned on his heel and strode along one of the paths.

"Where are you going?" she called after him. "You're supposed to stay here."

"You stay here," he yelled, without looking back. "I'm going to find Flash!"

Chapter Twelve

Zoe watched Oliver vanish into the park, her heart thudding. Max had clearly told him to wait at the zebra field. But was there really any need for both of them to wait here? The more people looking for Flash the better and Oliver knew Tanglewood really well. He'd know all the places Flash might be hiding.

She walked over to the fence and watched the zebras. Candy kept wandering around the field, braying anxiously for her foal, which made Zoe's insides churn.

"Please don't let anything have happened to him," she whispered to herself, closing her eyes. "Please let someone find him."

Zoe nibbled at her fingernails, worry coiling and uncoiling in her stomach, and once again her eyes stung with tears. Oliver was right – this was a total disaster. And it was nobody's fault but hers.

Candy called again, letting out stressed-sounding yips and brays, and came over to the gate. Zoe brushed her fingers along the zebra's bristly mane.

"I'm sorry," she murmured. "I didn't mean for this to happen."

She gazed around, wondering which direction the foal had taken. Glancing down at the thick mud beside the path, she saw a smudged hoof print facing towards one of the paths. Frowning, Zoe kneeled beside it and touched the mark. The mud was still soft, wet from the early morning rain, so the print must be fresh. And she had a strange feeling in her stomach, a certainty, that it belonged to Flash. Urgently, she scanned the ground for more hoof prints and spotted a faint imprint in the grass a little way from where she kneeled, then another. Without stopping to think, she followed the trail.

It led her away from the main area of the park and towards the meerkat enclosure, where the builders had stored their machinery behind wooden fences at the edge of the forest. The trail of hoof prints in the grass verge stopped. Eyes narrowed in thought, Zoe looked around. And then she saw it – one of the wooden panels hiding the excavators was disturbed, leaving a gap just big enough for a child to slip through. Or a curious little zebra…

Zoe walked forward, craning her neck to see around the painted wood. An exacavator loomed over her like a sleeping monster in the gloom. Could Flash have come this way? There was nothing on the other side, nothing except trees and a road that cut through the forest.

She was about to turn back when she saw a few

strands of coarse brown-black hair caught on the wood, hair that looked just like Candy's. Could it belong to Flash?

Excitement tingled through Zoe's veins as she crept forward. Her eyes straining for a glimpse of black-and-white stripes among the machinery and trees beyond, she hardly dared to breathe.

A flurry of movement to one side caught her eye and something grabbed her arm. "Stop!"

Zoe yelped and turned to see Oliver crouched low, glaring up at her. He tugged her down to his level and she saw behind his anger that he was worried.

"Flash is just behind that JCB," he whispered, pointing at the vast yellow machine blocking Zoe's view of the forest. "I've tried getting closer but every time I do, he thrashes around. I don't want to spook him."

Biting her lip, Zoe checked her watch: half an hour until opening time. "We have to do something," she insisted. "Time is running out!"

Pulling away from him, Zoe crept forward until she caught a flash of white around the edge of the JCB. Flash was standing still among the trees some distance away. She narrowed her eyes and squinted hard – was it her imagination or were his flanks heaving? There was a sheen over his withers too, almost as though his coat was wet. Zoe frowned. Oliver was right – he looked scared. But if he was scared, why hadn't he bolted?

She watched for a moment longer, noticing the strange way Flash was standing. "His tail is caught on that tree," she said suddenly. "That's why he's not moving. We need to free him!"

Chapter Thirteen

Oliver stared hard at Flash for a few seconds.

"Okay, you might be right. But every time I went near him, he threw his head around. Those tree branches are quite low, he could catch his eye on them."

Zoe shivered at the thought of the pain that might cause.

"What we need is a way to distract him," she murmured. "Then you could slip around the back and untangle his tail."

"The only thing that distracts Flash is food," Oliver said, "so unless you've got a secret stash of hay in your pocket I don't think that plan is going to work."

Zoe smiled. "I can do better than hay," she said, reaching into her pocket for the carrot she'd picked up at the food stores. "I've got a zebra's favorite treat."

Oliver glanced down at her hand and almost smiled, before he seemed to remember who she was.

"Okay. Take it slowly. Wait until I'm around the other side of the excavator before you let him see you. And hold out the carrot so he can smell it right away."

Biting her tongue, Zoe nodded. Oliver might be talking to her as though she was Rory but they needed to work together – now wasn't the time to start another argument.

"Okay," she said. "Be as quick as you can."

Oliver crept towards the back of the excavator.

Zoe waited for what felt like an age before she eased forwards, keeping her gaze fixed on Flash. The foal didn't seem to have spotted either her or Oliver yet. So far, so good…

A movement to her right caught her eye – Oliver was in position. He was directly behind the foal, making it less likely he would be seen. With a careful nod, Zoe held the carrot out.

"Here, Flash," she called softly. "Want a treat?"

The foal's ears flickered forward and he took a step back.

"There there," Zoe murmured, keeping her voice low and comforting. "What have I got for you, boy? I told you I'd bring you something tasty, didn't I?"

Flash's eyes rolled back into his head as she stepped nearer, and for a heartbeat Zoe thought he would panic. But she stretched out her arm, murmuring comforting words, and he settled down a little. Behind him, she could see Oliver edging closer. She was almost close enough to touch Flash now and she could see foam around his mouth.

"Poor boy, you're really frightened," she said, feeling another surge of guilt. "I'll have to find a way to make this up to you, won't I?"

Breaking off a chunk of carrot, she flattened her hand and held it underneath the foal's nose. He snuffled gratefully at her skin and the carrot disappeared into his mouth. She loaded up her palm again and let him eat. Encouraged, Oliver stepped quickly forwards. A loud crack filled the air as his foot snapped a branch. Flash's eyes rolled backwards and he looked panicky, but Zoe placed a firm hand on his wet, sweat-covered neck.

"Nothing to worry about," she said in a calming voice. "It's just Oliver. He's come to help you."

The foal quietened. She offered him more food and while he slurped and snuffled his way through the carrot, Oliver reached out and untangled his tail from where it was snagged on a wickedly sharp-looking branch.

"There," he said in a shaky voice. "All done."

"So far so good," Zoe said, letting out the breath

she'd been holding. "Now to get him safely back to the field."

"We'd better hurry," Oliver replied. "It's almost opening time."

With a jolt, Zoe glanced at her watch – less than twenty minutes to go! Briskly, she ran her hands up and down Flash's legs, checking him for injuries.

"I think he's okay," she said. "Come on, let's get you back to your mom."

Oliver ran on ahead to let the keepers know the foal had been found. Zoe couldn't help feeling a little proud of herself as she used the last bit of carrot to lead Flash home, one hand steadying him as they walked. Her dad and Max were waiting with Oliver, their faces alight with anticipation. It hadn't been easy coaxing Flash into letting them help him but they'd done it. If only she hadn't left the gate unlocked in the first place…

Max smiled as he led Flash into the field. "Let's reunite you with your mom."

Candy trotted towards them, braying joyfully.

She touched her nose to Flash.

"Awwww!" Zoe and Mizbah said, at exactly the same time and everyone laughed.

"Nice work," Mr. Fox said as more keepers arrived, "especially Zoe and Oliver. I suppose we'll overlook the fact that you ignored your instructions to wait here."

Zoe eyed her father nervously but he didn't seem to be angry. No one did, in fact, they just looked relieved that Flash had been found. She watched as Max bolted the gate and snapped the safety lock into place.

"I'm really sorry," she said. "I should have taken more care over locking the gate after myself. It won't happen again."

Max and Zoe's father looked at each other.

"Ah, about that," Mr. Fox said. "It turns out you weren't the last person to go into the field. I ran into one of the plumbers while I was looking for Flash. Apparently he went in to check the new water troughs one last time and didn't lock the gate properly. He admitted he had the safety lock in his pocket."

A whoosh of relief washed over Zoe as she took in the words.

"Oh!" she exclaimed. "Thank goodness!"

Beside her, Oliver cleared his throat. "I suppose I'm sorry too," he told her, in a voice that only sounded a tiny bit grudging. "I shouldn't have said the things I did. You were really good with Flash, he trusted you much more than me."

"Because I had the food," Zoe said, grinning. "But thanks anyway."

All around them, people were bustling around, talking into radios and straightening up their uniforms.

"Look," Max said, with a smile. "There's your mom and Rory."

Rory was running along the path towards them, an enormous beaming grin on his face.

"Zoe, I saw a flying squirrel," he called. "It was so furry!"

She kneeled down and swept him into a hug. "Awesome!"

Mr. Fox high-fived Rory and then checked the time.

"Places, people! We've got ten minutes to spare."

Everyone scattered, hurrying back to their stations.

"Oh, but I didn't finish my list of jobs," Zoe exclaimed, suddenly filled with panic. "There's still loads to do."

"I could help," Oliver said. "If you like."

Zoe turned to stare at him. "Really?"

Oliver shrugged. "We didn't make a bad team when we rescued Flash."

"I'd like that," she said with a smile.

Dad glanced at his watch one last time and took Mom by the hand.

"Ready?" he asked.

"Yes," Mom said, holding out a hand to Zoe. "Ready?"

Zoe looked at Rory, who let out his loudest lion roar.

"We're definitely ready," she said.

With a final nod, Mr. Fox lifted his radio and grinned.

"Okay, HQ, open the main gates. I now declare Tanglewood Animal Park open!"

Zoe and Oliver stood at the edge of the zebra field, listening to the delighted laughter of the crowd as Flash entertained them.

"He's a natural," Zoe said, as the foal posed for the cameras.

"You mean he's a show-off," Oliver said, grinning. "He loves being the center of attention."

Zoe laughed. "He's going to have some competition when Tindu arrives. Everyone loves tigers."

"True," Oliver said. "But for now, he's Tanglewood's number one."

Zoe gazed around, taking in the hordes of visitors, the animal-balloon stall and the furry life-sized Tanglewood bear mascot with one of the junior keepers inside. The smell of fried onions floated on the breeze from the hot-dog stand a short distance away. She thought of all the hard work that had gone into getting the park ready for this moment, all the worries and fears and stresses and arguments that had troubled everyone at the park. There'd been times when she'd wished her family had never moved here but that feeling had vanished. Tanglewood was her home now and there was nowhere she'd rather be.

"I can't believe we actually made it," Zoe said. "I keep wondering when I'm going to wake up."

Oliver glanced sideways at her, eyebrows raised. "You think this is a dream?"

Smiling, Zoe shook her head. "No, I don't. I think it's a dream come true."

The End

Visit www.edcpub.com or
www.usbornebooksandmore.com
for more
TANGLEWOOD adventures!

How well do you know TANGLEWOOD?

Take our Junior Zookeeper quiz!

Q: Why is Candy, the zebra, being kept away from the rest of her herd at the start of the book? *(Turn to p20 to double-check.)*

Q: Which super-cute striped-tailed male creatures show each other who is boss by having a smelly stink fight? *(You'll find the answer on p19.)*

Q: Which silvery carnivores have just moved in to Tanglewood? *(Page 14 will tell you.)*

Q: Which animal loves being with its friends so much that it is illegal to keep one on its own in some Scandinavian countries? *(Find out which pet prefers to live with friends on p89.)*

Q: All penguins come from cold countries: true or false? *(Find out on p106.)*

Q: What do flying squirrels use as a brake when they want to stop gliding? *(Check if you're right on p94.)*

Q: Zoe helps feed creatures who love to swallow their dinner whole. Name them, and extra points if you can remember the breed! *(Dive into p105 for the answer.)*

Q: Zoe knows she must not help the little baby zebra foal to stand up once he has been born. Can you remember why? *(Remind yourself on p84.)*

Q: Blue, red, orange, yellow and green... What's this rainbow-colored creature at Tanglewood? *(Page 114 has the answer.)*

Q: Zoe has a bowl full of sweet potato, melon, carrots and parsnips: which animal is she about to feed? *(To see who's having dinner, go to p49.)*

Zoe's Zebra Fact File!

BORN WITH STRIPES! Baby zebras, or foals, are born with their stripes, although they are brown and white at first.

BIG BABIES! A baby zebra weighs an average of 66 pounds. That's the same weight as the average ten-year-old!

UP AND OUT! Baby zebras are speedy learners! They are able to stand on their own as early as 15 minutes after being born, and can walk – and sometimes even run – within an hour. This is VERY important for zebras in the wild, so they can keep themselves safe from predators such as leopards and cheetahs.

ZEBRAS ARE LIKE SNOWFLAKES! No, really, they are, because every pattern of zebra stripes is unique – just like a person's fingerprints, and like snowflakes!

ZEBRAS STICK TOGETHER! In the wild in Africa, zebras live together in herds. By traveling together, their stripes act as camouflage, making it difficult for hungry predators to pick out any single zebra to chase.

VROOM VROOM! Zebras can run as fast as 35-40 miles per hour. When chased, a zebra will also zigzag from side to side, making it harder to attack it.

WHAT DO YOU GET WHEN YOU CROSS A ZEBRA WITH A Seriously, though, zebras can be bred with other types of horses. A zorse is the baby of a horse stallion and a zebra mare. A zony is the baby of a male zebra and a female pony. But best of all is a cross between a zebra and a donkey, called a zonkey or a zedonk.

Meet Tamsyn Murray, author of TANGLEWOOD ANIMAL PARK!

Where did you get the idea for Tanglewood Animal Park? Anyone who knows me will tell you I'm animal crazy! I'm also lucky enough to live very close to an amazing wildlife park and I visit it a lot. One day I started thinking about how great it would be to have a zoo of my own and – BOOM! – Tanglewood was born!

If you could be any animal, what would you be? I think I'd quite like to be a red panda. They always seem very contented and chilled out when I see them at my local animal park. They're cute and cuddly, too, and can sleep way up high in the trees.

Of course I wouldn't mind being a tiger, although I'd spend all day looking at my reflection!

If you could be a keeper for any animal, which would you choose? Oh, this is a tough question. You're sure I can only choose one? Hmm... I think it would probably be one of the big cats; snow leopards or perhaps tigers. I'm fascinated by the pattern on the snow leopards' fur, and by their super-long, furry tails. But I also love the tigers' stripes and the tufty little white spots at the very tip of their ears. I wouldn't be able to resist stroking them, though, so maybe it's better that I'm not a big-cat keeper!

What's your favorite animal story?

I couldn't possibly choose! *Black Beauty* by Anna Sewell, told entirely by the horse, is a classic. There was a series called *The Animals of Farthing Wood* about animals journeying in search of a new home which was HUGE when I was younger. But if you really made me choose, I'd have to go for *The Diary of a Killer Cat* by Anne Fine, because Tuffy and his adventures still make me laugh now.

Acknowledgments

Goodness, I owe so many people for this book! Enormous thanks to everyone at Paradise Wildlife Park for putting up with my endless (often peculiar) questions with patience and for sharing their brilliance and expertise. In particular, I need to thank Lynn Whitnall for being so generous with her time and resources, James Cork for his zebra advice and Steve Penrose for the snow leopard tips. Any mistakes are absolutely down to me.

I couldn't have written this book without the support and advice of superstar Jo Williamson – as always, thank you for being my agent and my friend. At Usborne, I owe a huge debt of gratitude to Team Tanglewood: my wonderful editor, Stephanie King, whose author TLC is second to none, and to Jenny Tyler, Rebecca Hill, Anne Finnis, Sarah Stewart and Becky Walker for ensuring this book is exactly what it needs to be. To Amy Dobson, Hannah Reardon Stewart and Megan Graham, for working their PR and marketing magic. Thanks also to Hannah Cobley and Amy Manning for designing the cover and Sarah Cronin and Hannah Cobley for designing the inside of the book so gorgeously. And thanks to my American editor, Carrie Armstrong, and EDC in the USA. Special thanks to Chuck Groenink for his illustrations.

Closer to home, I must thank the amazing Elaine Penrose, without whom I'd sell a LOT fewer books – a bookseller/event organizer extraordinaire. Thanks to Wormley Primary School, Oakmere Primary School and The Wroxham School for hosting Tanglewood writing groups to help me get animal inspiration. Huge thanks to the Arts Council England, who gave me a grant so that I could take the time to concentrate on writing these books without worrying how I would feed my family. And lastly, thanks to my lovely children, T and E, who each support me in their own special way and have allowed me to visit zoos for many years while pretending it was all for them...

Usborne Quicklinks

For links to websites where you can watch video clips about lots of different animals, find out about the life of zookeepers and test your animal know-how with quizzes, games and activities, go to the Usborne Quicklinks website at www.usborne.com/quicklinks and enter the keywords "Baby Zebra Rescue."

When using the internet, please make sure you follow our three basic rules:
• Always ask an adult's permission before using the internet.
• Never give out personal information, such as your name, address, the name of your school or telephone number.
• If a website asks you to type in your name or email address, check with an adult first.

To find out more about internet safety, go to the Help and advice page at the Usborne Quicklinks website. We recommend that children are supervised while using the internet.